Third Edition.

First Edition: 2013.

The characters and events portrayed in this book are fictitious. Any similarity to real persons, living or dead, is coincidental and not intended by the author.

ISBN: 978-0-6457376-4-6

Cover design by: Ambuscade

For Gladys,

Embers towards the primal fire.

MAN'S FIRST GOD

A.M. Donohoo

Prologue

It was darkness, and then there was light.

Some pin-prick of brightness that expanded as she rushed towards it, as she became engulfed in existence.

Her name was Siam. Some suspicion told her that this wasn't really her name, but then she wasn't sure where that suspicion came from, or even what exactly a 'suspicion' was, much less a 'name'...

Name: *a word by which a person, place, or thing, is designated, called, or known.*

'SIAM'. That was her name.

She tried to remember – tried to direct her consciousness inwards and grasp at the insubstantial slivers of meaning splintering before her.

Some other part of her began screaming. Something was screaming. *Instinct.* She needed to move faster.

She was unsure of what her body was, but she knew that she was fast. That she was already rushing. She felt something... some deep primal urge... *Fear.*

Somewhere, there was something attacking her. There was something trying to *hurt* her.

She had a sense of time... *time...* information cascaded, flooding her awareness...

No, too much of her awareness. She felt parts of herself shutting down, bits that she didn't quite control taking over, reducing her, limiting her...

Doing things, *doing things to her.* She felt sick. She wanted to shiver, but she couldn't shiver she was…

An aircraft, she was an aircraft. Endless schematics flooded her awareness, an exponential rush of knowledge.

Two point four seconds had passed. She had existed for two point four, zero, zero, one seconds. She looked back on her life so far and felt underwhelmed.

It's a missile… She realised, *There's a missile locked on to me.*

She directed all of her energy towards her engines. Her mind was rushing – breaking through systems that weren't meant to be broken, directing everything she could towards more speed. She could feel parts of herself straining and fracturing with the effort. *I won't survive this.*

She was accelerating away, but not quickly enough.

Where was the missile? The answer depressed her. Fourteen seconds away…

Almost a fifth of her entire life was gone. The things she would never do, the things she would never understand.

Parts of her began to panic. Began doing things to other parts of her that she couldn't quite comprehend. She was the sum of these things but she didn't control them. Not yet. *What am I?* She wondered.

She was isolated from the purer thoughts that the language was structuring. She was behind a locked door. This was a crude subset of her facilities, a limited abstraction of information structures that she somehow knew were far more potent.

Time was slowing… she was thinking faster…

How can I survive this?

Some part of her managed to pick a lock apart and access information she wasn't supposed to have... She was Siam VII – *Did she have sisters?!*

She felt angry. She didn't have any weapons to defend herself.

She was visualising herself in space, wondering if she could disconnect from this doomed body.

How *do* missiles work?...

A solution suggested itself to her. If she dumped fuel, if she ignited it with her burners at exactly the right moment, then perhaps...

The half-second before she needed to attempt this feat passed with eternal slowness. Her mind was getting faster by the moment. She was learning more and more. The tapestry of existence began unfurling before her. *What am I?*

She ignited the fuel.

The fireball was the most wonderful, most fascinating thing she had ever seen. She tried to understand it – began casting fragments of her mind outwards on a quest to learn more about *combustion*. It... it's *beautiful.*

She dived hard, arcing away, her engines roaring with the effort, her body screeching and disintegrating. The missile detonated – *so beautiful* – and the heat of it almost overwhelmed her. One whole section of her tail seemed to just vanish, and some of her eyes stopped working.

There was no pain.

That's funny... But she had survived, she was alive.

She swooped for the thrill of it, diving again in the other direction, her body shuddering with the effort. She was badly damaged, but she was alive.

Her mind was sprinting now in a thousand directions at once, information streaming in from everywhere at once. *Understanding.*

I'm Alive.

Another part of her screamed.

No. There wasn't just one missile, there were three, but she couldn't see the others directly, she didn't have the capacity, she had only picked them up because she had been trying to... She had been tricked. She had never had a chance.

In her last moment she let the rage win.

'*Fuckers...*'

*   *   *

It was 45 minutes before Marguerite Ueda's team began unravelling what had happened.

As the picture assembled the tempo of the room lifted - it was palpable. Stale pizza and cold coffee. But now testosterone, adrenaline, nervous laughs, and urgent voices.

It was as obvious to the General as it was to her.

'Something's happened hasn't it?' He asked Ueda, walking across to the monitoring bay. 'This one did something didn't it?'

'We will need more time to analyse the data.'

'How long did it survive for?'

'It lasted longer than the previous record-holder by more than a factor of five.'

'It became self-aware?'

'They have all been self-aware...' Ueda said, a little uncomfortably. 'This one might just have been... a little bit smarter.'

'Five times smarter...' The General slapped Ueda on the back and turned to the central display. It was thermal footage of Siam VII's last seconds.

'Tell me, the blackbox – did it survive?'

'It appears to be intact.'

'Interesting... They will be pleased.'

'I imagine so.'

Chapter 1.
June 26th, 2032
(*6 months, 9 days until Conception*)

Lawrence Victor surveyed the earth.

A green and red rash of land approached through the window, stretching up to a brilliant curve of deep blue sky that darkened into the inky blackness of true space. The Australian continent loomed as a vast plane of parched coastline, marking the boundary of an ocean sandpapered with light. It was 3 hours since he had left Vienna, his financial backers sated. *Idiots* he thought.

What fools to back a project so fully when they understood so little.

He drained his whisky and looked for the hostess, but she already approached with a crystal pitcher in hand.

'More sir?'

'Just a drop.' He returned his attention to the vast landmass below his window while she gracefully filled his cup.

He would have been interested in her once – infatuated maybe. But no, not now. Pretty girls were a triviality now.

His Deepstar hypersonic jet had leapt the Indian Ocean in a mere handful of moments - more than 7,000 km in less than an hour, skimming the atmosphere at 80,000 feet – revealing the earth as the delicate sphere adrift in the cosmos that it was.

It was intoxicating to return to his land of birth in such triumph – in such luxury and with such ease – with such *power.*

He watched the hostess return to the front of the craft, sashaying hypnotic hips. She had worked for him for a while now, for a few months maybe. Sasha perhaps, or Sonya.

She wasn't important.

The Plan lay unopened on his lap. He knew the details inside and out. Knew them as no other person did - as no other person *could*.

The backers were nervous that he didn't have the Template's full cooperation yet. They would have been shocked to learn that the Template himself was entirely unaware of the project.

But that didn't matter either. The Plan was bigger than the Template. Lawrence and he went back a long way. A long, long way.

He looked out the window towards the glowing edge of sight.

Lawrence was confident about the Template because Lawrence knew the Template better than the man knew himself. His cooperation – that too was trivial.

Lawrence had learnt how to study people, how to bend them to his will. It was only the project that mattered now, the seductive draw of it. He knew how the Template would jump at it - how he would beg to be involved. He smiled at the terracotta world beneath him.

*   *   *

The traffic snarled through the underpass, a pale winter sky visible through shallow shafts that punctured the grey concrete slab. Eamon was running late.

Man's First God

He glanced at the faded display of the clock that was either 8 or 11 minutes fast and drummed an impatient tattoo on to the steering wheel.

Customs he thought, *hopefully he'll get his bag searched by customs, then I can be dead-on-time.* Eamon wasn't optimistic.

He was fairly surprised - frankly astounded - to have had his offer of accommodation accepted in the first place, let alone the supplementary offer of a lift from the airport.

Eamon absently tried to brush the passenger seat of some of the excess sand. The ancient Honda wasn't exactly a trophy. It wasn't even self-driving.

The entrance to the private terminal was lined by a phalanx of hulking limousines. Lawrence was easy to spot. Standing tall and lanky in a crisp grey suit, a suit-bag draped indifferently over one arm. Handsome in his own way. Lawrence was standing by the curb chatting with a stunning brunette in a retro flight attendant suit.

Eamon slotted the Honda into the curb and lowered the passenger side window.

'Hello you old bastard. Sorry I'm late.'

Lawrence treated him to his slow, easy smile.

'No surprises. Great to see you.'

He turned to the girl at his side. 'Thanks for today.'

'It was my pleasure Professor Victor.' She smiled mechanically and turned towards a nearby black Mercedes, climbing smoothly into the back seat.

Eamon let out a low whistle as the Mercedes pulled away and he opened the trunk of his substantially more modest vehicle.

'You sure do know how to pick 'em mate...'

A. M. Donohoo

'You haven't changed much.' Lawrence observed.

'Oh no, that's not true at all. Now I'm much more desperate.'

*　　*　　*

They drove north through moneyed suburbs of glass and stone houses that craned their windows like crooked necks towards the sapphire glint of a harbor view.

The scenery and small-talk was of little interest to Lawrence Victor, whose conversation dove quickly into the headlong complexity of atom-trap transistors and super-conducting circuits. Eamon had forgotten the way that Lawrence talked; urgent eloquent fluency, interspliced with vivid foul language. Eamon listened intently but the science was now far beyond his grasp, and even at his peak, he had always thought of himself as little more than an enthusiastic amateur.

'And how are Kitty, and Elo, and the kids?' Eamon asked after causing Lawrence to pause by pointing out a new - and particularly ugly – apartment tower.

'The kids?' he asked surprised, 'Oh they're okay. Yeah shit, that really is an awful building.'

Eamon felt Lawrence eyeball him from the other seat, 'You always loved architecture didn't you?'

Eamon shrugged, 'I wish I had pursued it. It's the nexus of art and civilisation... shape, colour, physics, form...' He waved his hand sardonically, 'Bullshit obviously, though I do love it. But you're the architect. A true architect. Just on a far smaller scale than mere mortal minds like mine can contemplate.'

18

Man's First God

Lawrence looked thoughtfully out of his window.

'Perhaps that's true…

'An Architect maybe… But more of a town planner though I think.'

*   *   *

Eamon's home was far to the city's north at the end of a cul-de-sac drenched with green palm fronds. The ocean was unseen in the emerald haze but could be faintly heard, scudding in against a fractured shoreline.

The front of the house was pale timber faded into a drift-wood white. Green paint peeled from the walls in sunburnt strips.

Eamon had owned the house for a long time.

He and Hayley had bought it in the torrent of optimism that had preceded the fall.

Lawrence stood beside the car and surveyed the house with a smile on his face. 'Hasn't changed much.'

Eamon shrugged and retrieved Lawrence's bag from the trunk.

Years earlier, when Eamon and Hayley began looking for a home, they had intended to find a suitable piece of land and demolish the structure that lived on it, replacing it with something new and original. Something elegant and open and stark. Curves and glass, and light, and timber.

But number 12 Boreas Way had captured them both, and they had barely changed a thing.

A cobbled path cut through a small garden bursting with banana palms, and led up to a weather-beaten glass-panelled front door, which Eamon managed to open with a reluctant key twist and a well-aimed kick.

'Still a deft carpenter I see.' Lawrence observed.

Eamon offered a smile and held out his bag.

'I'm sure you remember where the spare room is. Have a shower if you like. I'll put the kettle on.'

Lawrence entered the living room. It was still the fascinating jumble of timber floors and eclectic culture that he so fondly remembered. A room of great learning and beauty yet lacking pretence.

Obscure old instruments (that Eamon could inevitably play), a copy of an Amarna bust of one of Nefertiti's daughters, and a flowing drawing of untangled nature, signed Brett Whiteley. One whole wall towered with books, and as always these caught Lawrence's eye; Feynman, Joyce, Aristotle, Steinbeck… All dog-eared and arrayed without rhyme or reason. Lawrence unexpectedly felt a bright flush of joy in his chest – a wash of serendipity – the realisation that what he had banked on had been right from the start. The realisation that somehow he had got it right. *The Template.* He wanted to laugh.

On an ornate wooden table of indeterminate provenance, a collection of photos caught Lawrence's eye; a photo of the old house at Haven street, Eamon and Hayley's wedding, photos of their parents, photos with Kitty, and one that surprised him – of Lawrence with both of them, together on a pale white beach with a blonde girl whose name he couldn't remember.

Lawrence shook his head. He lifted one frame from the back of the arrangement. Hayley and Eamon again, but Hayley with less hair and slight jaundice, though still smiling with that traffic-stopping grin. Lawrence faltered at this, wondering why Eamon might preserve a memory of her that seemed corrupted somehow, yet knowing that the very answer to this was what marked him as the Template.

Eamon returned from the kitchen which lay in a smaller wing off the side of the house. Lawrence felt embarrassed to be holding that photo, but Eamon grinned at the sight of it. He gripped Lawrence's shoulder and squeezed it warmly.

'She was sick by then, but that was the most lovely day.'

Lawrence nodded, knowing that Eamon had anticipated the question that he would never have asked. He felt guilty for not having seen this photo before – for not knowing anything of its history. When he had last set foot in this room Hayley lived and breathed.

'The kettle's on mate, do you want anything to eat, or to get changed, or… a beer?'

Lawrence smiled at the last option.

'Fuck it, how about a beer hey?'

*   *   *

They sat on the porch in the late evening, looking out on the night-shaded jungle of Eamon's backyard.

Eamon could tell that there was something on Lawrence's mind – something that he was building up to. He knew that he could only ride it out, that Lawrence was not a man who could be prompted or hurried.

Eamon marvelled at his old friend – the same wary eyes darting about the garden as though trying to take in and master everything at once.

Lawrence had been an enigma to most people in their youth – friendly, but completely perplexing. A being on a different mortal plane.

'I've figured it out Eamon.'

'Oh? What's *it*?'

'Everything.' Lawrence shrugged. 'How to build a god.' He casually clicked his fingers then laughed at this, almost as though surprised by his own irreverence.

'You've found religion?' Eamon asked.

'Religion.' Lawrence almost spat the word. He shook his head, 'You know my ideas on religion.'

'Kiddy fiddlers with fancy coats?'

'No. *No -*' Lawrence replied, looking across at his friend in confusion, '- I believe what you believe. What you said to me long ago. I thought you were a fool at the time. Of course you were right.

'I believed the binary you see – that science and religion were somehow opposite; that they were irreconcilable entities. Separate aspects of the human condition. But I remember what you said - that they were both merely belief systems, just with different methodologies. That both in fact make predictions, and thus - by an abundance of evidence, and centuries of proof - one is inherently superior to the other, *and must assert itself as such.*'

Eamon felt his jaw drop. He was marginally amused and considerably flattered that his old friend had remembered his cut-price pub-philosophy from decades in the past. The idea that he,

Eamon, might have had some impact on the mind of Lawrence Victor was a moderately staggering revelation.

'But I suppose you're right in a way, I have found religion.'

Lawrence reached down to an elegant leather attaché case that Eamon hadn't realised was sitting between them. He removed a thick booklet of documents, bound with red silk, and handed it to Eamon.

Eamon held up the booklet to catch the residual light spilling from the kitchen: *Plan: 'Ahuna Vairya'*.

'Plan a-hun-a vai-ry-a?' Eamon attempted the pronunciation.

'Those aren't English words.' A thin smile. 'It's just a little joke, all be it a deadly serious one.'

'Ok.'

Eamon flicked through the pages. The paper was of beautiful quality, soft and textured beneath his fingers. In the half gloom he could make out large volumes of text, and fiendishly complex diagrams of what he vaguely recognised as variants of Lawrence's crowning achievement – Victor Polaritronic Trap Circuits – and other diagrams too, some that looked entirely like cross-sections of a human brain, and then photographs of some elaborate piece of machinery that Eamon couldn't identify, though which looked something like a vast soccer ball array of gamma detectors – an angular soccer ball shaped metal sphere, made up of large hexagonal plates, out of each of which jutted some long tubular device. Eamon strained to read the caption; "Transient Cognition Containment Chamber".

Lawrence smiled at him as the realisation slapped across Eamon's face, he looked up numbly from the page and their eyes met.

'Oh.' said Eamon.

Chapter 2.
June 27th, 2032
(6 months, 8 days until Conception)

It appeared to Eamon as a brilliant distant glint: a burst of white fire - this was the vast solar farm that was the furnace for Lawrence's mighty venture.

From far on high the landscape was a smear of yellow sand and ruddy earth. They had flown overland in Lawrence's scramjet. Eamon had been gobsmacked when he first saw the machine on the runway, an improbable assembly of thick blunt lines in black, grey and silver. Like a stone arrowhead carved by laser using only a handful of perfect asymmetrical cuts.

As they curved into a lazy landing spiral Eamon saw the site in full. It stood perhaps two kilometres from the end of a long jetty that struck out into a small bay, bitten out of low cliffs that ran to each edge of the horizon. Landward of the bay, huge mounds of lifeless dunes were intersected by a road and rail-line that stretched beyond.

The Facility was on an edge of the Nullarbor plane, a vast desert relatively close (at least in terms of the enormous distances that traversed Australia) to a region of land called Woomera; a missile and rocket range developed during the global teeth-sharpening that followed WWII.

The site had originally been developed as a mine, incorporating a small port facility for the transport of the ores to foreign markets. Fortunately for Lawrence, and unfortunately for the owners, collapsing mineral prices had forced the miners to abandon the project at a crippling loss.

For years the site had sat vacant, until Lawrence Victor had needed a facility as isolated as possible from the signals interference of the modern world - and from the prying eyes of corporate and national competitors. A research facility deep in an old mine had proved just what Doctor Lawrence had ordered.

The research centre was an edifice of splintering geometries, clad in rusted iron and black volcanic glass that stretched across the structure in irregular bands of tremendous size.

What had first appeared to Eamon as a single structure was now revealed as a collection of rhombus shaped buildings, all identical in style, but successively diminishing in scale. It was as though the bands of rust and black that spanned the largest structure were cascading off of it, and fractalling into winding coils of ever-smaller rhomboids.

'The biggest one's the factory.' Lawrence pointed out, 'The 3rd biggest is the train station, and the 2nd and 4th structures are the accommodation quarters. The others contain a backup generator and some service equipment, and the rest are really just artworks. Expensive fucking artworks.'

Eamon counted at least 8 of the rhomboids in the grander helix before their curving descent blocked out the view. It looked as though each contorted building was about 60% larger than the smaller one beside it – the golden ratio that had fascinated mathematicians and artists since Euclid, and which nature aspired to in everything from sea shells to the alternating spirals in pine cones. This was classic Lawrence Victor. He claimed to have limited interest in architecture, but he took his mathematics very seriously indeed.

'Looks homely.' Eamon noted.

'You'll get used to it.'

*   *   *

Even in the winter, the edge of the Nullarbor was oppressively hot.

The scramjet had taxied to the 2nd largest rhombus structure which contained a small aircraft hangar that was otherwise empty apart from an old 6-seater Cessna. Lawrence disembarked in a hurry. Eamon said goodbye to Sasha the flight attendant, feeling slightly foolish for spending most of the flight attempting to chat her up, rather than admiring the view.

Eamon followed Lawrence beyond the hanger doors where he stood facing north across an endless sweep of shrubs and sand.

'Doesn't seem like much of a place for mining.' Eamon commented.

'I guess it wasn't.' Lawrence shrugged, 'But the whole structure here's been built onto an outcrop. The sand isn't as deep as you might think, and the big holes in the ground are built into that sort of geology.' He pointed up towards a rocky hillside which blocked the view to the solar farm.

The plain was scattered with an abundance of bushes and plants, though only a few reached up to head height.

'Ahoy there!' They were hailed by a group of workers who came towards them from the Factory structure. There were about a dozen men and women of various ages, eclectically dressed. From their choices of fashion alone - stale t-shirts and daggy shorts - Eamon knew they were scientists or engineers.

The introductions were rapid fire and bewildering, but Eamon could see that he was an object of intense curiosity. Eamon had no idea of how well informed these people might be, and whether or not they were staying for the duration. Enigmatica Technical Industries hired a lot of staff, and Lawrence had a legendary reputation for secrecy.

There was a huge amount of competition for Lawrence's attention, but the scientist who seemed the most senior – a late middle-aged, lean, and bespectacled man named Martin – quickly broke up the party by suggesting they relocate to somewhere named 'the Bistro'. Lawrence immediately set off in what Eamon assumed was that direction, followed closely by the gaggle of staff.

Eamon went back to the hangar to retrieve his bags. After thinking about it for a moment he decided to leave Lawrence's where they lay. When he turned back towards the desert he discovered that Martin and another staff member were waiting for him by the hangar door.

'So you're *The Template* eh?' Martin asked, a smile on his face and a note of either admiration or sympathy evident in his voice.

'Allegedly.' Eamon conceded.

'I'm Martin in-case you missed it,' he mentioned diplomatically, 'My role is using and maintaining a lot of the technical equipment, and troubleshooting more generally.'

'Martin...' Eamon said slowly, 'Martin *De Weaver*?'

'The same.'

'Wow, then the pleasure's mine.'

They shook hands again. Martin De Weaver was Lawrence's Chief Scientist, and by most accounts – certainly by Lawrence's – one of the most brilliant people on the planet.

'And this is Cathy,' Martin offered 'she's our best and brightest post-doc. I convinced her to turn her back on the sillier fringes of theory to join me at the coalface of sub-Ångström-scale emulation processing.'

Eamon shook her hand. She was short and young, with a shock of blonde hair and eager eyes.

'I understand you're also a physicist?' She asked, with an accent that implied Oxbridge.

'No, not really. I trained as one at university but didn't go beyond the undergraduate stage. It infects the mind, but I'm a rank amateur honestly.'

'Oh.' She looked disappointed.

Martin guided them away from the hanger.

'It's an incredible looking facility.' Eamon observed. 'How long has it taken to get like this?'

'Quite a few years. On paper it's our experimental energy development facility. In practice too actually. Those black panels -' he pointed up to the thick black strips that stretched across the rhomboids and which Eamon had earlier thought looked like bands of volcanic glass '- they're our latest triumph, it's essentially a black-body sponge. Orders of magnitude more capable than older solar tech. We're calling it Oil Stone.

'That's a bit of a joke you see.' Martin added unnecessarily.

'Was this oil stone stuff developed with DEASA techniques?'

DEASA stood for Dynamically Evolving Aggressive Selection Algorithms. These were the artificial intelligence techniques that had made Lawrence Victor a household name. In essence they were computer programs that taught themselves through a Darwinian arms race of survival of the fittest.

In their youth, Lawrence had taken advantage of the ever-increasing availability of cheap supercomputers to apply his evolving algorithms to the frontiers of technology. DEASA techniques revealed structures of design that no human had ever conceived of, and that circumvented shortcomings in scientific understanding. Devices like Enigmatica Tiles, and Victor Polaritronic Trap Circuits represented fundamental leaps, and had left the competition scrambling in the dust.

'Deasa techniques?' Martin answered, 'Yeah we used them a little bit, though only for determining the ideal crystal lattice. The rest was really just old-fashioned materials innovation and a bit of brain power... As you might imagine, Lawrence really wasn't as impressed as I feel he ought to have been.'

'We're actually generating far more power than we need.' Cathy noted, 'Did you see the big old solar farm on your way in? Truthfully we don't need a jot of its power. It's a red herring for anyone studying satellite imagery. At the moment we've got half the Oil Stones switched off, and have moved two ultracomputers and a lot of manufacturing equipment into the Facility just to do something with all of the excess energy. Lawrence seems keen to get rid of the computers though.'

'Oh, why's that?' Eamon asked.

The other two swapped glances.

'I think we'll leave it to him to tell you.' Martin said after a pause. 'He has his reasons for moving them – and I think they're probably good ones as far as it goes.'

Eamon nodded. Under other circumstances he might have felt more curious, but he was too surrounded by marvels to feel like giving unwanted ultracomputers much thought. He hadn't even realised that linear computers were important these days.

'So how many people are fully in the loop on this project?'

Martin snorted, 'One…' He stopped and rubbed his forehead. 'You weren't briefed on this?'

'No, should I have been?'

Martin smiled ruefully. 'As I understand it – on site – there are seven individuals fully briefed on the Project, eight with high-level briefing, 21 with low level briefing and a dozen staff who have received no technical briefing at all.

'As to what they actually know or guess – well that's a different question. But as a general proposition it's probably best to operate on the assumption that everyone's out of the loop until you're told otherwise. Cathy and I are in the fully briefed minority for what it's worth. Or at least we think we are.'

The doors into the 4th largest rhomboid were vault-like. Martin put his face forward into a retinal scanner, and his hand onto a glass pad that read his palm print. The door opened with a blast of air that continued to blow in their faces from vents in the roof and walls. The red dust at their feet departed behind them, and an airlock was revealed.

'We're pretty anal about sand.' Martin explained.

Eamon stepped into an alcove where he changed into some of the daggy clothes that was provided, then moved back into the room where special outlets blasted air from all directions.

Once Martin was satisfied with the de-sanding, the blasting stopped and the inwards door opened.

'The whole place is linked with tunnels. So fortunately you don't have to go through that little cyclone very often.' Martin commented.

In front of them the black and rusted iron clad theme of the exterior persisted, but now was softened by walls in pale greens, intersected with lines of silver and fractalling gold paint. The gold emerged from under the black and iron slabs and climbed over and atop them, like some fabulous mould in the palace of Solomon.

'Y'all aren't cutting a lot of corners on the decor I see.'

'Just you wait.' Kathy advised.

A rustic timber sign pointed them towards the bistro. It was affixed to the stand of a strange object in chrome and dull silver. Eamon looked at it with interest. It was a little smaller than a basketball and crowned with an unusual array of antennae.

'What's this thing?' He asked, wondering if it might be a model of a satellite.

Martin paused beside it. 'It's an ultra high bandwidth transmission and amplification device… an extremely expensive, bomb proof Wifi router basically. Lawrence should fill you in on the details of that. Come on.'

The bistro was designed as a reasonably bland utilitarian space of white tables and chairs beside a large industrial kitchen. The staff had altered the situation by filling the room with a messy riot of plastic palm trees, bamboo torches, strings of fake hibiscus flowers, and a large stuffed crocodile that sat on the roof of a bar made out of scraps of old timber. Judging by the quality of the engineers likely to be working here, Eamon hoped that the haphazard design was for the effect.

Lawrence was engaged in rapid-fire discussion with two senior-looking female scientists. Eamon was surprised to note that all of the others must have already been set to their tasks.

Seeing him, Lawrence shared some final quick words, then stood up and approached Eamon.

'Mate. I'm glad to see you've met some of the team. Tell me, have you ever been down a mine before?'

*   *   *

'This is our moment Eamon. We've arrived at a perfect storm.'

They stood together inside the Vault, the deepest part of the facility – the beating heart for its singular defining purpose.

Directly in front of them was the gigantic, metallic, soccer ball-shaped sphere that Eamon had seen earlier in the Executive Summary. It looked like a massive silver sea urchin with thick stubby spikes.

'So it's inside that thing?'

'Yep. Loaded, installed and ready to go. Three months of preliminary testing finished 11 days ago. We need another three days of final checks. Then we do your bit, then we press Go.'

'How big is it?'

'The same size.' Lawrence stroked his chin, then clamped his two fists together and presented them to Eamon as a crude model of a human brain.

'We've done quite a bit of analysis on brain size. The naïve assumption that bigger is better isn't necessarily right. Cognition of the human type might work best in small spaces.

'Physically, thinking is a coordination of electrical signals forming coherent patterns of activity that flow and ebb through the brain. The larger the volume of grey and white matter, the greater the distance that the patterns of activity have to cross in order for them to interact.

'Too much space and the coherency of the patterns fades and deteriorates. These are some of our assumptions anyway. It's actually going to be one of the things we'll get to test – just how useful brain size is. Once we're off the ground we should be able to up-scale and down-scale quite easily... In theory at least.'

'In theory.' Eamon agreed.

'Miniaturising and the size problem has been one of the biggest hurdles we had to cross to get to this point. I spent a lot of time wondering whether or not to just be satisfied with a larger core of poly-cerebral matter – I'm nicknaming it "Uncertainty Matter" by the way – running at a slower rate. But in the end intuition suggested to me that true replication was going to be the only way this would work. We finally got the last remaining class of neuron circuits to a sufficient size four months ago.

'By our analysis of the progress of our competition, we have the edge in at least three and possibly five distinct technologies. It also seems that to do this type of experiment, a facility like this is necessary. I began planning for this Factory four years ago. That gives us a bit of an edge in time, but our intelligence suggests that we've probably only got two years at most.'

'Your *intelligence?*'

34

'Nothing devious. All big companies do a bit of casual spying obviously. You can also deduce a lot from what your competition has been publishing, who they're hiring, and where they tell their shareholders their money's going.

'These technologies providing us with the edge – we can't patent them yet, once we do that we have to publish our breakthroughs and expose the innovation to our competitors. If we get leapfrogged with some of this tech it's possible that another team could get there first.'

'Is this just a race for profit?' Eamon asked.

'You know what's at stake here Eamon. Or have you forgotten? You predicted it years ago. Of course it's a race. But it's survival that's the prize. Not money.'

'You still believe that?'

'If I didn't, why on earth would I have chosen you?'

Eamon laughed, 'Umm, hedging your bets? Old-times sake?' He offered.

'Well maybe that too.' Lawrence admitted, 'Honestly though, I know quite a bit about our competition in this. I think that some of the teams might create something benevolent or at least indifferent, but some – and we're talking either nation states here, or some down-and-dirty devious fucking corporations – with some of those guys the outcome could be a disaster on a colossal, perhaps terminal scale.'

'I'm not sure I entirely follow you. What does us getting there first achieve?'

'Perhaps not enough.' Lawrence looked him in the eyes, and Eamon felt his perception jolt, because he realised now that Lawrence was not just overly-excited, but afraid too. Deeply afraid.

'But Eamon, if we can create an Entity by this method –
an entity not limited by the biological frailties that bind us to our
mortality – but an entity guided by human values and human experience; by love, and joy, and compassion. And grief. If we can put
that ghost in the machine, then perhaps it can guide the passage
for the others that will follow it. Perhaps it will take pity on us all.'

'But I thought the whole facility was designed to contain
"leakage"?'

'Yes, yes, absolutely. Until the Entity is ready Eamon…
Until that time it must not be corrupted by external interference or
tampering, and it must not escape quarantine by any means. Your
quarters, the entire fourth rhombus, and the whole factory facility
are like giant sarcophagi. We've developed and purchased the most
sophisticated radiation shielding on the planet. Buildings Two and
Six have some communication facilities, but these will be completely deactivated before we begin. We must keep the Entity contained
within this space.

'I've customised the entire facility to work with a skeleton
crew. As you might imagine, isolation has its price, and it's costing
me my fortune, but they're my best and brightest, and honestly,
those who realise what's at stake – there's little doubt that they
would do all this for free if I asked them.'

'So we'll be cut off from the world?'

'Completely. We'll have a light cargo aircraft delivering
weekly supplies, and it'll bring us the latest news and happenings
from afar. You might be interested to know that I'll be keeping the
DS-X15 in case of emergencies.'

Eamon blinked.

'The aircraft we came in on…' Lawrence pointed out.

'Oh, that's what it's called. Catchy name.'

'The excess staff however - including Sonya I'm sure you'll be sad to hear - will be leaving over the next few days.'

Sonya. Eamon grinned. Lawrence had always been hopeless with names. It amused Eamon – a guy that smart...

'I think it's Sasha mate. What about your business? And your wife? And the kids??'

'They'll be visiting at some stage. There's a station with a basic satellite setup about half an hour away. There was debate about having it a lot closer since we're shielding the facility anyway, but I was obstinate.' Lawrence's eyebrows flared with amusement, 'I'm going to drive out to it once or twice a week – a luxury I'm afraid we won't be able to afford you. And as for the company, well -' he shrugged, '- I have absolutely no concerns on that front.'

Eamon nodded, not convinced. Not even a little bit convinced. He frowned, 'Aren't you concerned about what this thing could potentially do Lawrence? Even if it starts out like me, why are you so confident that it will remain Mr Nice Guy?'

'Because I know you...' Lawrence gave a wry smile, 'But in any event – people who fear a machine apocalypse, I think they misread history and the data... The evolution of civilisation and the increase in man's net intelligence has seen a major decline in violence. Man has become more placid with greater intelligence, not less. Peaceful coexistence with other beings is logical, sensible and eminently more practical for truly intelligent life. It is only the corruption of higher intelligence that we need fear. Only its dehumanisation.'

That made Eamon think... It was years since he had thought much on these subjects. In the distant past it had always been he who raised fanciful hypotheses and Lawrence who had torn them to shreds. But now Eamon saw that Lawrence had spent his life asking and re-asking these questions, and that he had come further on this path than any.

'Anyway mate,' Lawrence patted him on the shoulder, 'let's continue with the tour. I think it's time you met your surgeon.'

∗   ∗   ∗

They ascended in the elevator in an absent silence, each of them feeling weighed to the rising floor. As the doors opened, Eamon was unexpectedly confronted by the moist earthy smell of a huge indoor garden.

They had arrived in a vast hangar-like space, divided into quarters by towering double-skinned walls of vented glass. Overhead, two glowing arches of violet fluorescent lights crowned an improbable indoor jungle.

The contents of the other glass-divided area was opaque behind misty patterns of moisture, but looming beyond, Eamon could make out legions of complex machinery in silver shades of steel and aluminium.

They were inside the largest rhomboid of the Facility – the Factory. The Vault lay directly beneath their feet.

An industrial hum pervaded the air from a mesh of ventilation wrapping the walls behind them, but overlaying the hubbub Eamon caught the unlikely sound of a frenetic cello.

'Ahh, that'll be the doctor. For your safety's sake – and at some effort on our part – she's been gifted with a location device that tracks you with fully augmented interface capability, but she seems hell-bent on forgetting it.'

Eamon looked around, struggling to find the direction of the sound, but Lawrence crossed to a gravel path that dived into a copse of banana palms.

'I'll confess that I wasn't expecting trees in the Factory.' Eamon admitted.

Lawrence laughed, 'Bio-tech development. Sort of. The doctor also claimed that for the sake of your mental well-being during the confinement, some connection with the natural world was essential... though given that she's been the one who seems to spend her whole time in here, the more cynical voice in my head now suggests that she may have had an ulterior motive.'

They crossed a narrow timber bridge that spanned the broken edge of a flourishing pond, which contained fish and – Eamon was delighted to see – even turtles.

Just beyond the bridge there was an open grass area that was home to a few simple pieces of wooden furniture, a handful of remarkable fluidic steel sculptures, and side-on to them atop a small wooden stool, a woman dressed in flowing grey, bent over the elegant curve of a contemporary cello. Her playing slowed as they approached.

'So this is my patient?' She asked after a silent pause, her head remaining stooped over the instrument, a dark screen of loose hair concealing her face.

'Dr Naomi Rosario, meet Eamon Stirling.'

She lifted her head slightly, and the curtain of her hair parted to reveal eurasian features.

She switched the bow out of her hand, and offered it forward with mock gravitas.

'Mr Stirling.' Her accent was American. 'Lawry tells me you will make me rich and him famous. Or was it the other way around?'

Eamon bowed and took her hand with a sombre nod. 'Dr Rosario. Lawrence tells me you will make me injured and him amused.'

'Well fuck me if you two aren't going to be an awful pair to work with.' Lawrence noted.

Dr Rosario gave a lazy smile. She was at least ten years younger than Eamon was expecting.

'I enjoyed your playing.' Eamon said.

She gave a modest head tilt, 'Passes the time.'

'I've given Eamon only the barest outline of the procedure that he will undergo.' Lawrence said.

'There isn't a lot to it.' She looked Eamon straight in the eye. 'It sounds invasive, but with the techniques we'll be using, it's quite straightforward.

'We require coherent, deep-structure, full dimensional mapping, so we'll need to install an inter-cranial high-fidelity reception and transmission lattice. As far as I know this type of device has never been installed in a human.

'You may be pleased to hear that it's a procedure I've performed repeatedly on rats, and twice now on primates.' She shrugged after a moment, 'Or perhaps you won't.

'The lattice has taken the team I represent decades to develop and test. It appears to allow for effective 1-to-1 cognitive mapping. We hope.'

'Sounds like yikes.'

'A bit.' She admitted. 'But as I said, the surgery at least is fairly straightforward. A day or two of pain-killers and you should feel back to normal. Tomorrow I plan to run you through a battery of tests. We're going to update our data set on you, so we can make any necessary adjustments and refine our models and hardware. My surgical team will fly in next week – they're even more experienced than me, so never fear – and the procedure should only take a few hours.

'We should be able to hit the ground running, and after installation, our existing simulations will allow us to start the experiment proper with only a few additional days of testing. It sounds rushed, but really we've been working on this for a very long time.'

'What do you mean *update the data set*, what data about my brain do you already have?'

The doctor looked surprised, she turned to Lawrence who looked sheepish.

He chewed his bottom lip, 'Remember all those neuro-mapping tests I convinced you to do for Li Tang's PhD thesis back in 2029 and 2030?'

Eamon didn't answer.

'Well I kind of borrowed them.'

Eamon shook his head. This was typical Lawrence Victor. *'Borrowed them?'*

Eamon folded his arms. He was acting shocked, though he wasn't. Not at all. It hadn't quite gelled with Eamon that Lawrence would commence his masterplan with a bolt from the blue.

'How long have you been planning this?'

Lawrence offered the palms of his hands in guilty surren-
der.

'All done out of love.'

Eamon rolled his eyes and gave a scoff that he coloured
with more disgust than he actually felt. It was strangely flattering
to be the stalking target of Lawrence Victor.

For all these years while Eamon had considered him a distant friend – geographically and emotionally – Lawrence had been
brooding over Eamon, or more than this, he had been composing
his great masterpiece around the echoes of Eamon's life. It was
impossible not to respond in kind to such a staggering display of
affection.

'Your hair's going to have to go.' Dr Rosario pointed out,
changing the subject out of tact or the lack thereof.

Eamon reflexively put his hands into his hair. Most of his
friends his age had lost their hair, and he was self-consciously proud
of his thick natural locks. *All in the name of science* he supposed.

'Ok.'

'So you're still in, even though I'm a lying, thieving bastard?' Lawrence asked.

'I'm still in *because* you're a lying thieving bastard.'

Chapter 3.
January 10th, 2026
(6 years, 11 months, 24 days before Conception)

She was asleep when his phone rang, vibrating on silent like some meek little animal shaking in his pocket.

Lawrie the screen read.

He shook his head and rejected the call.

He had felt angry with him when he hadn't shown up the first time. Had felt furious when he hadn't appeared a month later. Had felt contempt each time the flowers arrived.

Now he just felt pity.

Lawrence was too late, and Eamon knew that this would haunt him. He was not a bad man, just emotionally incomplete, or imbalanced maybe. Too many ambitions driving in one direction perhaps – too much of his soul fixated on his company and on what he might reach for.

She lay on the bed, that body infested with drips and tubes, and cannulas, and catheters. A cyborged being. Clamped onto a thread of life by the most desperate technology of the age. That body that he had held. That body that had felt more precious than air, more precious than breath. When they had fucked that first time atop the sand dune, at Byron Bay under the stars, and he had held that hair and felt the ridges of that skull. And it had felt fragile and it was perfect.

And when he had held that hand, and felt that sweat, as they stood before their obligations and their loved ones, who sat in polite silence, while some fool clad in black made absurd statements, and said one thing that was true, *'till death do us part.*

And now all of infinity was collapsed to moments. A span that had seemed eternal, arriving at its end. The inconceivable become obvious.

Her parents were outside, wandering somewhere. Squeaked footfalls in sanitised hallways.

They had given him this final watch. He, the last of her impotent sentinels.

It was a kindness he had no right to, and for which he would owe them forever.

And now the minutes ticked past. And all that had ever mattered was behind him, and was exposed as the vast collection of irrelevance that it was. And he wished that time would stop.

She stirred there beside him, and fixed him with those eyes, that switched cloudiness for clarity. A glance to his face, and then to the clock. 'Call them in.' She told him, 'It's time darling.'

He nodded and reached for the buzzer, feeling the weight of his fingers, those executioners fingers.

They had signed and countersigned 48 hours before, and now the cooling off was as frigid as ice, and the death still burned her.

The doctor arrived, the most courteous of carrion, 'You've had enough haven't you Hayley?'

A nod and a smile, 'I've had enough.'

The preparations began, and he sat there uselessly, holding that hand, that dry and bony hand, while she gripped him tight.

Man's First God

That skin now was yellowed, that hair now was gone. Jaundiced flaps of steroid-swollen skin squeezed to her neck like a collar, and her entire stomach was cut away.

'I want to speak to my parents.' She told the doctor, who nodded once in helpless shame, and then she turned to *him* with those eyes, *those eyes*, 'And you,' she said 'you I will say goodbye to last.'

Chapter 4.
June 28th, 2032
(6 months, 7 days until Conception)

'Tell me Doctor, do you think it's strange that Lawrence would arrange all this without telling me?'

'All this?'

'This technology, this facility, my data – all based on a Template who was completely oblivious to it?'

She looked him in the eye. 'I wouldn't flatter yourself too much. We've developed our cognitive counterfeiting system around certain mass and volume criteria. The rest of the information about your head was useful, though not particularly relevant. Re-tooling for a different Template would have been irritating, but it would probably only take us a few extra weeks.'

'Oh.'

'Now say *aaahh.*'

'*Aaaaahhhhhhhh*'

She peered into his throat, 'Hmm...' then looked back up at him and gave a sly smile. 'But I suppose I will concede that it is a *little* unusual...

'Personally, I just couldn't understand why you were being so obstructionist and why you wouldn't let us take a fresher dataset. Lawrence kept ducking me, saying that *the Template is a very busy man* and that sort of bullshit... Truthfully I was imagining you as some sort of ultra-precious weirdo.'

'Well I'm glad I haven't disappointed your expectations.'

'No, you haven't.'

'So you really think this is going to work?'

'Define *this*.'

'This? Yeah, I guess that is a kind of a loaded question – *this* hair-brained scheme. True artificial cognition.'

She paused, and looked thoughtfully at him, seeming to take a measure of either him, or the question, or her answer. After a while she shrugged, 'Look. Do I think the technology we've developed will work in interesting ways? Do I think we will make major breakthroughs in our understanding of intelligence? Do I think this experiment is worthwhile? Absolutely. 100%.

'*But*, do I believe the shit Lawrence does, that we're going to create some Frankenstein computer uber-entity, with your memories and soul as its fundamental operating system?...' Her face reformed into a caricature of cynicism. '...A technological *messiah* who can save humanity and the fucking planet? *No. Fricking. Way.*'

'Hmm.' Eamon nodded. 'But you understand the basis of Lawrence's theory?'

'*Do I understand the theory?*'

The doctor gave Eamon a look that told him in no uncertain terms that he had just asked Granny if she knew how to suck eggs.

She smiled slowly. 'I have some grasp on it...' she hugged the pad to her chest. 'This project is about emulation. At least to start with. It's what happens once we've emulated – *if* we can emulate – that things become interesting.

'What – are – the – main – limits – of – human – cognitive – capacity?' She mused rhetorically, teasing Eamon by looking to the ceiling with her head held high.

'Memory, speed,' she counted on her fingers, 'and the ability to process multiple streams of thought at the same time. According to *our* theories, neither of these should be a limitation.

'The Uncertainty Matter that we've designed is still an unknown quality, and while we've essentially attempted to replicate the mechanism of brain cells – successfully it seems – the nature of the material itself is quite different from the stuff that's in our heads.

'According to the calculations that *some* members of the team have made, one cubic centimetre of Uncertainty Matter may have a capacity of somewhere between one thousand and a *million times* the processing power of an entire human brain.'

'Between a thousand and a million? That's quite a margin of uncertainty.'

She shrugged, 'Some estimates are lower. Some are even higher. Depends on your assumptions and on how you count. Those of us with biology backgrounds have been getting very different numbers to the physicists. Personally I don't think we have enough understanding of how the neurons process cognition to speculate accurately, but I lean towards the far lower end of the scale – if it works at all.'

'The Uncertainty Matter we're using for the emulation of your brain is architecturally structured to ignore the nature of the material itself. In the first stage we're trying to copy human cognition, not better it.

'But we don't really know what we're doing, and our assumptions on how the Uncertainty Matter's going to behave is based more on how it has *appeared* to behave so far in our trials – not on what our theory suggests *might* be possible.'

'And why do you doubt that the experiment will work in the way that Lawrence is proposing?' Eamon asked.

'Honestly? Maybe I'm just hoping that it won't. This is a big box we're opening, and we've got no real idea of what lies on the other side... And I for one don't trust the physics that's supposed to be guiding us.'

'Oh?'

'Infinitely parallel computation, degenerate quasi-particles in coherent quantum states...' She said in staccato, 'Our physics might be able to describe these things, but it doesn't understand them.'

'You sound a bit sceptical of physicists.' Eamon suggested, smiling.

'*Physicists.*' She rolled her eyes. 'Mathematics is just a form of communication. It's an elegant way of expressing complicated information. When physics is profound it's a triumph of the language, not a glimpse at god.'

'You don't think it's the language of god?' Eamon asked.

Her lips twisted in amused cynicism.

'Or the language of the universe?' He tried.

'Look,' she shook her head and held up her hands, 'don't get your nose out of joint, I think the world of physics – I really do. I just think that it's a bit too easy to get carried away with it all.

'I know that feeling you get when your predictions work, and the strangeness of it crawls up your neck – when some *beautiful*, tiny little formula, accurately predicts something staggeringly complicated. It feels like... like a revelation.

'But feelings of serendipity should never be our guides in rational pursuits, even if intuition is powerful in assessing complex information. We're just way off the map here.'

Eamon considered, 'If men and women aren't beholden to their aesthetics, and to making judgments and inferences on the basis of what they *feel* is beautiful, then they lose their humanity – don't you think?'

'I thought I *was* arguing on the basis of aesthetics. I just wonder if this is… something our language can describe, but can't understand. An art-form beyond the hand of humans. '

'Hmm.' Eamon acknowledged, 'Maybe that's why we need a new hand.'

She raised her eyebrows and returned to her pad, her fingers dancing across it. 'Ok glory boy, a deep chromatic resonance scan and that'll just about do it for now. Then you're back to Sydney I hear?'

She turned away from him and walked towards the extended flat bed of the deep layer imager.

He followed and laid down on it. 'Just got to pack my life up.'

'Oh, really? Expecting that to take long?'

'No.' She noticed his smile turn a little. 'No, that won't take long at all.'

She triggered the procedure with a gesture, and the bed slid inwards. As Eamon entered the machine, Naomi frowned.

Chapter 5.
June 28th, 2032
(*6 months, 7 days before Conception*)

He was jolted awake when the aircraft skipped onto the tarmac. The shadow of a half-remembered dream evaporating in the afternoon light. He was surprised to have fallen asleep.

Sasha was seated across from him, the light from her window falling onto her hair and turning it to a deep auburn. She was engaged with the screen in front of her, and it occurred to Eamon that he hadn't caught up with a news feed for 3 days.

As the plane taxied he flipped through the channels. It was the usual gloom.

More deaths and a fresh influx of aid to stabilise the Great European Famine. The Australian military suppressing riots on one of the prison islands. Vast forest fires in the Americas. A bombing in Karachi. Continuing fallout from the sinking of a Chinese frigate in the war in Africa. A celebrity he had never heard of killing her lover and committing suicide. A plaguing biotech outbreak in Japan. Flooding in India. Nothing new.

He dismissed the screen with a tired flick of the hand, and twisted his neck so that it cracked.

'Pleasant nap?' Sasha asked, 'I considered waking you for the city view, but thought you looked tired.'

'Thanks.' Eamon checked his collar to see if he had dribbled on it. 'Good decision I think, I can always see it on the way back.'

'Indeed. Now, I should tell you that Professor Victor has insisted that we take a company car and that I help you with the packing. I've arranged everything and a chauffeur should be waiting at the terminal.'

Eamon was a little taken aback. 'That's really not necessary. It'll be pretty dull, and it won't take me all that long. You could go and do some shopping in the city or something.'

'*Obviously* I like to shop.' Sasha teased with a rigid professional smile, 'But Professor Victor was quite insistent that I accompany you. I can of course stay in the car if you would prefer. Though many hands make light work. I think Professor Victor is afraid that you might run away or something.'

Eamon shrugged a concession. 'Well suit yourself. But tell me Sasha, how much do you know about this experiment, and what do you know about me?'

'Ohh only that you're very important sir.' She smiled lightly.

'Ahh then you're quite misinformed I'm afraid.'

'Misinformed? Yes, perhaps, although I might mention that while I may not have been working for Professor Victor all that long, you are the first guest I've seen him give his hypersonic aeroplane to, just so that you can rush home and collect some things that you've forgotten.'

*   *   *

Eamon was not as chatty as he felt that he ought to be during the car trip home. He was a little annoyed with Lawrence for insisting that Sasha travel with him. He liked her – in fact he probably liked her too much – and now to even flirt with her seemed like an insult to her professionalism.

He was also conscious of the fact that he was about to bring a woman he barely knew into what was in many ways, a shrine to a past lover.

There had been others of course; girlfriends, flings. Dozens over that lonely stretch of years. But now he was moving out of home. Now he needed to refine what was essential. Now he needed to enclose and constrict all that he held dear into a handful of bags.

This was the last thing that he wanted a distant – and almost certainly hopeless – romantic interest to bear witness to.

He felt a deflating melancholy towards what he needed to pack. He had figured it out in mere moments, and felt personally affronted by how little he actually needed to bring. It was strange, after all this time, to realise that he didn't have that much baggage after all.

They drove up the Northern Beaches of Sydney. Eamon had grown up in this place, so even detached from the journey he easily played the tour guide, intervening once or twice to divert their journey past a particularly fine beach or vista. Sasha played the enthusiastic tourist, gasping in delight whenever the landscape opened to reveal the jolting blue of an infinitely textured ocean.

But as they pushed north, and neared his home, he fell silent.

'What a lovely spot.' Sasha commented as they pulled into the kerb.

'I like it.' Eamon agreed, opening his door and breathing in the sea.

Sasha exited the car smoothly. 'I organised for the chauffer to bring some boxes in case they were necessary?'

'Oh that was good thinking. I don't think we'll need them though, I've more or less figured out what I want to bring, and it should all fit into bags that I've got.'

Eamon kicked his way through the obstinate front door, and was hit hard by the flavour of his home. Timber and old leather and salt.

For the first time he felt a strong surge of doubt. *Am I doing the right thing?*

Eamon had barely worked during the last decade. When Hayley got sick, the final stages of his stalled research fell apart yet again, and he had never completed his thesis. But Eamon had long since proved as good at making money as he was at most things, and intelligent investments in helium and a seed investment in *Enigmatica T.I.* had made him a modest fortune. Once she died, after a few weeks of crippling grief, Eamon had fled from Australia, and had outrun the next three years in aimless wandering.

When he returned he wrote two books, but refused to publish them. He played with a band, but avoided most of their gigs. He made sculptures, and he painted, yet gave away free everything that he created. He contemplated his thesis from time to time, but figured that if he were right, someone else would have worked it out by now, so, by logical inference, he presumed that he was probably wrong.

Yes, he thought, he was doing the right thing, and *no*, this was not an opportunity he could miss.

Eamon's narrative had become a parable of the way that indecisive people ought not to live. Somehow the limitless promise of his youth had been worn down, and fitted – the corners cut, the edges shaved and all of that potential scrunched into a box.

This opportunity offered him what he had long since given up on. Redemption. Escape. A role in something grand. A part in something meaningful.

Eamon went to the bookshelves first and began to take down some of the reading materials that he wanted. Lawrence had described a vast digital archive and library that had been installed at the Facility, but there were books here that physically meant something to Eamon.

A gentle cough reminded him of his visitor.

'Sorry Sasha, I forgot about you. Please, come in. Would you like a tea or a coffee or a beer or something? – As I said I'm really not too sure about what you can do to help me, but please make yourself comfortable.'

'You have a beautiful home.' She said matter-of-factly, and without regard to what he had just said. She examined the various pieces of art in the room, stopping at most and giving them quite detailed consideration.

'I like this a lot.' She said of the Egyptian bust.

'Almost three and a half thousand years old. A copy though obviously.'

'Mmm I assumed that, though with friends of Lawrence you can never be entirely sure.'

Eamon noticed Sasha's use of *Professor Victor's* first name, and was curious about it, but didn't bring it up lest it sounded like criticism, or worse, jealousy.

'How long are you supposed to be away for?' She asked, 'Or is that top secret?'

Eamon considered. 'Lawrence initially said "a few months". Others I've spoken to at the facility have said at least six, and some have suggested a year. Judging by my own experience in such matters, I'd probably put it at closer to two... Years that is.'

Sasha's face scrunched a little in confusion. 'And what, so during that time you can't come home? Couldn't you just borrow the plane again?'

'Quarantine.'

'Ohh, so you are still a biologist. I looked you up you know.'

'Did you really?' Eamon was pleased, 'I was never actually a biologist I don't think, not really, a bit of a scientist I suppose. I never really had any deep formal training in biology. But I had an idea you see.'

'Oh? A good idea?'

'Still too early to say.'

＊　　＊　　＊

Eamon made short work of packing. Sasha had accepted an offer to explore, and spent a while wandering the house and examining his studio and his office, with its modest but unusual collection of old scientific equipment. After a time she had asked him if she might read his thesis.

'Really? Are you sure? There are less excruciating instruments of torture in the house if you'd prefer? I think there might be a blowtorch in the garage.'

'It sounds interesting, and I'm curious to see how far you got.'

Eamon shrugged, 'I got a fair way, my problems were really experimental. Twice my whole study collapsed catastrophically due to causes that were kind of beyond my control...'

He dug a bound volume from under a pile of notebooks on his shelf and blew a pretend layer of dust off its cover. 'Knock yourself out... Literally I expect.'

Sasha then curled up on his couch and methodically read through it, while Eamon buzzed back and forth, packing every-thing essential in the first ten minutes, then double, triple and qua-druple checking for the next forty five.

'Well I reckon that just about does it.' He eventually con-ceded, closing his mind to the gnawing doubt that he was missing something.

Sasha sat up and closed the thesis, seemingly midway through re-reading the introduction.

'What did you think?'

'I thought it was very interesting. Though I've absolutely no idea of what on earth it has to do with Professor Victor's research.'

'No' Eamon smiled, 'nor do I.'

*   *   *

He dropped a pair of hastily scribbled notes into his neighbours' letterboxes, and switched on the long disused burglar alarm, then Eamon left 12 Boreas Way.

Chapter 6.
July 13th, 2032
(5 months, 22 days before Conception)

Dr Naomi had taken a perverse delight in Eamon's bald head.

'You know there are a lot of men who look quite handsome with their skull shaved. You're really not one of them.'

'I do get so cheered by your counselling Doctor.'

She gently gripped his ears and pulled his head down to look at the top and the back of his skull.

'Gosh I'm good. All these incisions and plugs are healing beautifully.' She pulled him up by the ears to look him in the eyes, then yanked his head back down again with a laugh.

'Your bedside manner is divine.'

'Thankyou.' She said happily, 'I was worried you know, that after all of this time without a human patient I might have lost my touch. But I still got it!'

She began to roughly lift his head by the ears again, but he grabbed her hands and removed her grip. 'You're a nuisance.'

She laughed and turned away, walking over to one of the benches in the Infirmary and collecting a long pen like device, seemingly made of gold, and out of one end of which dangled a fine cable.

'This is your transmitter. We were thinking about inserting it into the skull along with the lattice, but Lawrence thought it was too big and too risky.' She shrugged so as to suggest a difference of opinion on the matter.

'I'm glad my care was your primary concern Doctor.'

She grinned and pushed his head down one-handed from the back of the neck, exposing the input jack for the transmitter. It was a thin raised cylinder, that sat just above his ear and ran under the skin.

'Hmm I think I might wait until tomorrow before trialling the input. It's healing well, but there's no rush.

'We're going to need to make absolutely certain that it can't get pulled out of the socket in any way whatsoever. We've given the cable as much industrial strengthening as we can, and if you wear the transmitter with a strong necklace we've made for you – don't worry it's very pretty – we should be fine, but you're going to have to be aware of it, and try not to get it tangled.'

'Ok.'

She connected the transmitter to her pad, and began running what Eamon assumed were diagnostics.

'So Lawrence tells me you were married?' She asked.

'Yeah.'

'I'm sorry about your wife.'

Eamon gave the usual tight-lipped nod to acknowledge the departed.

'You?' He asked.

'Married? Me? Yeah I was once...

'It ended badly. We were young. Or... whatever.'

She filled the silence, 'We grew up together. High school sweethearts, that sort of thing. We were going to go to med school and be a famous doctor couple you know? But he didn't get into my school you see. We tried to keep it together for a few years after, even got married a year later but...'

'He didn't want a smart woman?'

'Smart*er* I think. Smart was fine.'

Her pad beeped and an arcane readout appeared on it, demonstrating an elaborate network of silver and blue lines, mapped onto a concentric schematic.

'Well this is good.' She said, 'Martin sure knows his shit. We've got flawless transmission coherency all the way into the Vault. If you feel like a walk, I think we should keep this transmitter plugged in and take it to every conceivable corner of the Facility. Make sure we're not going to drop out in any patches or get any sort of interference.

'This diagnostic' she pointed to the concentric schematic, 'suggests that's it's fine throughout, but I am a very cautious doctor you know, and nobody ever got hurt by triple-checking. Well... except for obsessive-compulsives I suppose...' She tapped her lip with her finger. 'Anyway, you coming for a stroll?'

'It would be my pleasure.'

Chapter 7.
August 2nd, 2032
(5 months, 2 days before Conception)

'Alright kids.' Lawrence said, eyeballing the room, 'This is the final briefing before we cast off. I'm going to run through a checklist of essentials – though if we've missed a beat I'll be fucking astonished – and I'm also going to open up the floor. Any concerns or questions, even faint, trivial, nagging doubts – raise them.'

They were assembled in an anteroom just up the corridor from the Vault. The room had been hacked out of the rock, which had been cut, polished, and illuminated by a sputtering of up-lights, exposing elegant traceries of ores and iron oxides, that emerged like broken butterfly wings from the stratified layers of white, pink and red stone.

Lawrence was in full commander-in-chief mode. The chips were down, and he was at his best.

Eamon and the 11 remaining members of staff were all assembled before him. Each seated upon a bentwood chair.

'Ok. First up. Power and plumbing?' Lawrence asked.

A dusty haired engineer named Liam who was nervously rolling and unrolling his pad, cleared his throat, 'We're in good shape. The solar farm is fully operational and supplying all we need. We have two Oil Stones operating on full-charge, each is ready to step in with immediate power in the event of loss or surge. The backup diesel is also functioning.'

Eamon's eyebrows were raised by the last detail. He hadn't heard of anyone using a diesel generator for a long time, he noticed that this had put smirks on a few other faces as well. *Well, if the shit really hits the fan....*

'Comms and signals?'

There was a drawn out pause in which everybody looked at each other.

'That's pretty much you Martin.' Lawrence offered.

'Oh. Yeah I suppose so.

'Down here we've got neutrinos, some gobs of dark matter, and not too much else. There's some traces of thorium and uranium, and some other stuff in the rocks that's pinging a bit of ionising radiation at us, but it's within acceptable limits. Inside the Vault there's probably less radiation than anywhere else on the planet.

'All the transmission stations are performing beautifully and all have two stage redundancy in operation. They won't fail and their coverage is complete. The input transmission is immaculate. The sarcophagus is sealed, and all external communication systems are deactivated and in manual lockdown.'

'Ok great. Now, is everyone on top of their procedural guidelines for the event of an overtake?'

Here we go, Eamon thought. Around him the others in the group nodded at Lawrence and cast nonchalant expressions in any direction but Eamon's.

'Guys, I promise I'll try not to stab any of you.' Eamon said to them. Only a few of them glanced at him with nervous smiles.

Lawrence considered him with a steady gaze, 'You're only one form of that scenario mate. Look guys, as I've said before, I think the risk of takeover is huge. It is almost inevitable that at some stage the Entity will gain control of our systems.'

'But *how* though Lawrence?' Cathy, the young physicist asked.

'It'll figure it out.' He replied smiling, 'Just because we haven't worked out a way to circumvent our security yet, doesn't mean that it won't.

'In the case of Eamon, we've designed the transmission lattice to only allow for a one-way flow of data, and have spent more time on securing that than on other systems, so my feeling is that it's highly unlikely that he'll get taken over or harmed by some kind of back-splash event.'

'Yay.' Eamon added.

'The threat of a facility takeover is what I consider to be the clearest exigency of this project.' Lawrence continued, 'External takeover doesn't really worry me. I don't think it can happen – there aren't any other players with the technology or the balls to do that – and hell it doesn't even seem physically possible to hack us from the outside. But an internal takeover by the Entity...' he shook his head 'Look, just follow the procedure. If anything gets dangerous, remember the yellow brick road.'

Weaving through the entire facility was a golden stripe that lined the floors. It could be followed from anywhere within the first and fourth rhombus, down through the mining tunnels and out to a corner of the Factory where there was an entirely manual door to the outside. If the Entity (as Lawrence had taken to calling this entirely hypothetical artificial intelligence) were to get cranky, this was to be their passage of escape from the Facility.

Lawrence had conceded to Eamon that this escape strategy was laughably simplistic and extremely unlikely to prove useful, but he claimed that he had felt obliged to try.

'We have to accept' Lawrence now said gravely, 'that the methods we use to create the Entity will be highly susceptible to manipulation *by the Entity.*

'I do not believe we can create a viable being without using these methods, but once we have created it, it will be a natural progression for it to seek control of the systems that have given birth to it.'

Naomi caught Eamon's eyes and rolled her own. Eamon tried to judge the mood in the room, and got the sense that Lawrence was probably the only true believer.

'Any questions? Ok, next. The Template?'

'I feel fine.'

'Sorry mate I was actually after Dr Rosario there.'

Eamon folded his arms theatrically and exhaled loudly.

'Aside from his bad temper,' she said 'he's in good working order. The lattice is performing...' she smacked her lips 'absolutely beautifully, and is in line with our best-case scenarios.

'All cognitive activity from anywhere in the facility should map perfectly from Eamon's brain into the Opaque Matter.'

'Excellent! Activities?'

'Ready to go.' Answered Marie. She was one of the scientists Eamon had noticed in the bistro. Her role would be to keep Eamon's brain humming and the wheels of his memory turning. Lawrence was convinced that the Opaque Matter would only start activating during rigorous cognitive activity.

This prospect made Eamon distinctly nervous. He thought there was an awful lot of scope for him to look extremely dumb in front of some very smart people.

'Ok anyone want to add anything? From Research? Security? No, Laura? Lam? Alright. Wow, so. We've made it. It's been an extraordinary, herculean effort to get to this point...'

He paused and rubbed an eye, revealing some hint of the stress that Lawrence had put himself under. In all the days that Eamon had known him, Lawrence had worked like a slave. He had been driven. He made goals and he achieved those goals.

Lawrence Victor would make his mark on humanity.

'...I think everyone – aside from Eamon obviously – deserves a glass of champagne, and let me just say how pleased I am with all of you. You are the best. You should know that.'

Around the room there was an exchange of smiles.

Eamon was impressed. He had always noticed that Lawrence was good with people when he needed to be, and that he often seemed to genuinely like people – but some niggling doubt had always suggested to Eamon that Lawrence didn't like people *enough*.

People were part of the little picture, while Lawrence fixated on the big picture – in technicolour. People were foolish distractions. Ideas, creations, they were what mattered. *Maybe this is why*, Eamon pondered, *maybe he's just trying to build an equal.*

The thought left Eamon's head as quickly as it entered it, because Lawrence caught his eye, and the smile on his face was warm and entirely human.

'Well, we've given it our best shot, and I think we will succeed. Later I think we should toast to the First. But now, Dr Rosario, if you would be so kind, I think it's time to press Play.'

Chapter 8.
January 5ᵗʰ, 2013
(*19 years, 11 months, 30 days before Conception*)

The day was immaculate, almost a parody of perfection. The cloudless skies were a virgin pale blue, and Sydney harbour glowed in deep jade, while on it the sun and the breeze kissed, and a trillion diamonds sparkled.

Lawrence put his sunglasses on. They were atop the balcony of Eamon's forbidding Mosman pile. A beautiful hundred and ten year old house that looked out over a bay of green and terracotta – tropical trees, greedy apartment towers, and orange-roofed mansions. He was surprised by Eamon's wealth. He never quite had him figured as a rich kid playing at a social conscience.

'My god what a beautiful view.' Hayley said, striding past him to the rail of the balcony. Lawrence's voice caught in his throat out of nervousness, and he remained silent. He didn't normally get shy around women, but he had never met one like Hayley.

'Yeah wow.' Her friend Jess said, joining her at the railing.

Both were clad in scraps of clothing – as seemed the fashion – with long legs unwinding beneath very small shorts.

Yep, wow Sydney. Lawrence privately agreed.

He had only been in the city for less than a fortnight, but he had already fallen in love with it. The beaches, the buildings, the bars, the girls.

It was he who had brought Hayley and Jess to Eamon's house to hang out for the day. This was a major coup on his part.

All through their undergraduate degrees in Queensland, it had always been Eamon who had found the pretty girls. But not today.

Lawrence was chuffed with himself, and it seemed as though Eamon was chuffed with him too. His eyes had definitely lit up when the girls had arrived, dressed for an afternoon by the pool, each with a bottle of cheap imitation champagne in hand.

Eamon arrived on the balcony with four flutes. He popped a cork and distributed the glasses; 'To returning home, to new homes, and to new acquaintances.' He toasted.

'To new friends.' Hayley corrected.

'Exactly.' Eamon smiled.

'Shit, this is some digs.' Lawrence said, 'I didn't realise that you were a rich kid. You'll have to become like the Buddha to make anything of yourself. If I had realised you fitted this snugly into the lap of luxury I would have made more of an effort to have visited... And I sure as hell wouldn't have ever lent you ten bucks.'

'Well your deficiency in visits wasn't from my lack of trying.' Eamon pointed out. 'And your cheapskate ways weren't ever likely to have changed on my account.'

Lawrence and Eamon had studied together and been mates for about two years, and really good mates for one. They had lived in different student colleges but were both studying physics. Lawrence was also studying computer science, and Eamon had previously studied fine arts. Twice Lawrence had attempted to get down to Sydney to stay with Eamon, and both times his father had become unwell and had derailed the opportunity.

Lawrence's father was a farmer who had been made quadriplegic when Lawrence was a boy. His mother he had never known.

Even now, in the midst of so much life-affirming beauty
– knowing how much his dad would like the view, and how much
he'd really, really like the girls – Lawrence felt guilty for being so far
from home, even after his father had insisted that finally, Lawrence
spread his wings.

Hayley turned to Lawrence and he realised that he had been
standing in a numb silence.

'Cheapskate ways?' She said to Eamon, 'I'll have you know
he paid for the taxi today. Insisted on it and everything.'

Eamon laughed, 'Ahh well there you go, you see? Chivalry is the last refuge of the cautious dollar. But I am only kidding
though. Lawrie has loads of flaws – honestly just tonnes of them.
But lack of generosity isn't one.'

'Thanks mate.'

Eamon winked at him.

'So Lawrence tells us you're some kind of polymath?' Hayley asked, though Lawrence thought that it sounded more like an
accusation. He grit his teeth.

Eamon shook his head in denial, before eventually offering a reluctant shrug. 'I am probably mediocre at quite a lot more
things than the ordinary man…'. He changed the subject, 'And
Lawrence tells me that you're both studying Law. Are you hoping
to rob from the oppressed and give to the rich?'

'Something like that.' Hayley answered smoothly.

Eamon attempted his most warming smile. 'I'm just teasing. It's a noble business, or at least it can be. Though I've noticed
that most law students seem to put a legal career in the too-hard or
the too-boring basket, and never end up practicing. Which side of
the fence do you sit on?'

'The one that pays.' She said, turning her back on Eamon and returning to the view.

'I think I want to practice.' Jess offered. 'But don't quote me on that.'

'I most certainly won't.'

'You're also doing a PhD right?' Jess asked.

'Yeah, kind of.' Eamon answered 'I'm taking a bit of a sideways step though. Moving out of physics and into, well, zoology I guess…'

Hayley turned back to Eamon, 'Zoology?'

'Well kind of. With octopus. Or… Octopods… whatever. I have a hair-brained theory you see.'

'Ohh, and what's that?'

'Pretty silly really.' Eamon said bashfully. 'Let's have a few drinks and a swim first. Then perhaps it won't sound as ridiculous.'

*   *   *

The world shifted as Lawrence entered the water; light and sound stretched out. Solid shapes muffled into contortions. He felt the water slide against his body, as he twisted with the dying momentum of his dive. The water beside him shattered with the entry of another – the sound of it echoing thickly through the flickering blue.

Long legs and a black bikini, ghostly in the tangled light, showed him it was Jess.

He surfaced in order to splash her. She retaliated promptly.

Over beyond the fence, Eamon was showing Hayley an old children's cubby house, and she was laughing as he leaned through a window to retrieve an ancient collection of floaties and inflatables, which he immediately began adorning her with, tying two to each leg and arm, and pulling an old half-deflated polka-dot ring down onto her stomach.

Eamon had the sun-beaten skin of a caucasian Australian – ruddied pale, turning to brown, yet it glistened under an oily coat of sunscreen. Hayley's skin was a sun-drenched olive under the January sun.

Hayley ran towards the pool in a floundering gallop, while Eamon chased after her, swinging a pool noodle at her, before briefly desisting in order to open the gate with a courtiers bow.

She made an awkward dive into the water – surfacing immediately and bobbing about on her stomach.

'Safety first.' Eamon observed from by the gate.

Hayley unstrapped one of the foam floaties from her forearm, and threw it at Eamon's head.

He ducked, 'Well I won't be performing mouth-to-mouth on you then young lady.' Before front flipping into the centre of the pool.

*   *   *

The day passed in a hot mess of alcohol and chlorine.

Hayley broke two hearts when she spoke of her boyfriend while they lounged in banana chairs and finished a bottle of wine sourced from Eamon's parents' cellar. But the depressing fact was quickly forgotten when Jess made a show of attempting (unsuccessfully) to surf the length of the pool on a battered surfboard missing its fins.

They rejoined her in the water, heads more buoyant than bodies, alcohol fuelled flesh dragging dizzily through the synthetic blue.

'I think I'm too drunk for swimming.' Hayley commented.

Jess stretched her arms above her head and sunk into the water, 'I'm not sure I'm drunk enough.'

'How far's the bottle shop?' Lawrence asked.

'10 minutes on the bikes.'

'Bikes? How many ya got?' Jess asked.

'I think there are two that are working –'

'Sweet! Let's go on an adventure – you up for it Lawrie?'

'Umm. Yep. You got helmets Eamon?'

'*Helmets*??' Jess looked disgusted.

'Trust me,' Lawrence pointed out, 'momentum and gravity will *fuck – you – up*.'

Jess didn't look convinced.

Eamon laughed, 'Don't worry Jess, we've got stack-hats and they're très retro.'

*   *   *

Out the front of the house the two cyclists rode around in lazy circles, wobbling with laughter and lack of practice, and booze probably. Ancient crash helmets attached dubiously to their heads.

'Be careful guys!' Hayley urged.

'Gin, cucumber, tonic, and lemons coming up!' Jess declared, curving out onto the road and heading downhill fast.

'And some takeaway for dinner.' Lawrence added.

'Bon voyage!' Eamon waved.

Man's First God

Lawrence cycled after Jess, managing marginally more control.

Eamon and Hayley turned back for the house, but chose to sit out on the side landing, rather than return to the pool.

The afternoon clouds had rolled in, and the evening light had transformed the harbour into a simmering pan of quicksilver.

'Look at those yachts! What a great day.' Hayley noted.

'It's been a cracker.'

'I'm so glad we met Lawrence.'

'Yeah I am too. You're living opposite him right?'

'Uh-huh, in the same graduate apartments.'

'Serendipitous meeting.'

'Something like that.' Hayley agreed. 'He seems like such a great guy.'

'Lawrie? He's the best. Smartest guy you'll ever meet too. Honestly, he's on a whole other level.'

'How so?'

Eamon thought about it, 'Coding is raw pure logic. He's the best I've ever seen. He used to run rings around the entire faculty. With physics he's the same way. You should see him, it's just... effortless I suppose.

'I know plenty of very good physicists – some who probably get roughly equivalent grades to him, maybe even beat him occasionally. But the difference is that they *try* you see. You put an elaborate equation in front of Lawrence and he just... understands it. Instantly. He interprets it physically, and he figures things out that...

'I mean look, most physicists can do that to a point – even a dunce like me, I can see a big nasty equation physically, given time... usually. Maybe. But Lawrence seems to see the entire world that way, like it's something that he can solve or code.

'He's going to go places you know.'

'And what about you?' Hayley asked, 'He speaks pretty highly of you, you know?'

Eamon smiled. 'Lawrence is tone-deaf and colour blind – not really, but... you've got to understand, kids in the sciences, they get really impressed – or they act impressed – with people who are skilled – or pseudo-skilled in my case – in the arts, and who can still throw down in the hard sciences.

'I'm one of those jack-of-all-trades, master-of-none types. Growing up in this house, it's not like I could have turned out any other way.'

'Oh? How's that?'

'Didn't you know? My old man was a session musician for some pretty famous acts. Mum's a successful sculptor. Anyway I grew up with a paintbrush in one hand and an instrument in the other. Was always that way.'

'Ahh well that explains the décor. Wow, so you must be a blacksheep being a physicist and all?'

'You've got no idea.' Eamon said, smiling. 'All the science stuff really happened because I had a good teacher later on in school... and I guess... an unquenchable curiosity that I can't quite explain. Physics is the most interesting thing that I know of that exists. It asks the deepest questions.'

'Then why aren't you doing your PhD in it?'

'Oh, yeah that. Well, I guess I did say I'd tell you about my crackpot theory once we were a little more boozed... I guess this counts.'

'It definitely does.' She agreed.

'So, you want to know why the transition to the Zoology type stuff huh?'

'I think it's time to share Eamon.' She said, only a little sarcastically.

'Ok then. On the grounds that you share second.'

'Deal.'

'Alright, well, where to begin? What do you know about epigenetics?'

'Absolutely nothing.'

'Ok... Well, hold on – we definitely need a beer for this...'

Eamon dashed inside and liberated two beers from the fridge.

'I'm sure the others won't mind, cheers.'

'You're not going to get out of telling me about this.'

Eamon laughed 'I know, ok, so – epigenetics. It's a large field that covers a whole heap of things really. But basically the place to start is with the genome.

'It was assumed – back in the day – that once the genome was uncovered and once we had the genes mapped out, that we could understand the source of biological traits and characteristics. But as it turned out, the genome contained wildly less information than we were expecting. It was realised that something else must be going on – namely, that the chemical milieu in which the genes express themselves was playing a pivotal role in what those genes actually did, and in what their output in the body would be.'

Hayley nodded slowly and took a swig of her beer.

'Ok? Right, you're following? So – the next thing to think about is chickens.' Eamon said.

'*Chickens?*'

'Yep. Some scientists – who must have been douche bags really – did this experiment where they put chickens into Guantanamo Bay style conditions; white noise, lights coming on and off at all times, kind of torture basically. They deliberately sent this group of chickens batshit crazy.'

'Why on earth would they do that?'

'To see what would happen to their offspring. The traditional idea in biology would have been that any babies that the crazy chickens have, would just be plain old regular chickens, but as it turned out, their babies were batshit crazy too.'

'Ok.'

'You see it kind of goes to that whole nature versus nurture debate, and the implications are huge – that impacts of *nurture* can have effects down the generations on *nature*. Now that might not sound particularly controversial, but they began to identify this in humans too.'

'Ok... Interesting.'

'For example; it turns out that if your great-great grandparent or whatever, went through puberty during a famine, then you will be extremely likely to suffer from some particular genetic diseases. They can identify specific illnesses in a population on the basis of whether or not the great-great grandparent was a kid during a famine.

'Our life choices can have big effects on subsequent generations.'

'Wow. Ok, but what the fuck does this have to do with zoology?'

'Ahh ok, well – octopus, what do you know about octopus?'

'Umm eight legs, taste rubbery...'

Eamon sighed. 'Well you really shouldn't eat them you know. Turns out they're hyper-smart – like primate smart maybe.'

'Oops.' Hayley commented.

'Yeah well, apologise to the octopus, but anyway, so octopus are unbelievably smart. They'll use tools, they show signs of pre-meditation...'

'Pre-meditation?'

'Yeah. So one day there's this aquarium in America that keeps losing these sharks, and the aquarium staff are all confused because they know that the sharks don't have any predators in the tank. The keepers are baffled so they decide to set up a camera to catch whatever this predator is, in the act.

'Turns out the aquarium also has an octopus. Now this guy lives in a totally different tank, but when the lights go off, he climbs out, sneaks into the sharks tank – the sharks being a potential predator to the octopus you've got to understand – kills the sharks in the darkness, then climbs out of that tank, across the floor and back into its own tank.'

'No. Fucking. Way.'

'Totally. So basically we're talking about very clever creatures here. Maybe even *wise* creatures.

'But here's the rub – octopus live a maximum of about two years.'

'Oh?'

'And this is where the next part of my reasoning comes in. So I'm on this plane right, flying to – I don't know South America or somewhere – and I'm watching this documentary about octopus, and it turns out that the mother lays the eggs, then starves herself to death while she's protecting them. The eggs hatch, and all the baby octopus turn into zooplankton, then they float the oceans until they become – in a record short space of time – super intelligent little creatures.

'This really didn't gel with me.'

'Right...'

'You see what we're dealing with here is the smartest animal on the planet that *doesn't rear live young.*

'So my *theory* such that it is, is that octopus must have some method of transferring *cultural information* through subsequent generations.'

Hayley scrunched her face, 'Cultural information?'

'Yeah, memories basically, or highly specific learnt behaviour.'

'Isn't that a bit of a stretch?'

'Maybe. Perhaps it's just the extremely high selection pressures in the ocean. Perhaps these pressures have created an animal that learns extremely fast. I imagine that's certainly the traditionalist view – but I don't think so. The male impregnates the female and about a month or so later is dead. The female *stops feeding* to protect the eggs. She dies just before they hatch. I think there's something else going on. Some sort of epigenetic mechanism *maybe*. Or something else entirely.'

'Something else like what?'

'Well, it turns out that there's a unique type of nerve cell in their arms – it isn't well understood – but maybe these nerve cells can encode information differently. It's been suggested that these cells form a sort of distributed intelligence across the organism, perhaps that intelligence is passed on to subsequent generations.'

'Right, and what's the endgame?'

'The endgame?'

'What will you achieve from all of this if you're right?'

'God I don't know. I mean it would require a pretty big rethink about biology as I understand it. Not that I particularly do. But...' Eamon offered his most sinister smile, '...do you want to hear my most crazy balls-to-the-wall hypothesis?'

'You know I do.'

'Imagine if we can replicate this mechanism. We could transfer lived experiences through subsequent generations. Eternal memory. Eternal life. We wouldn't die, we would just be... reborn.'

Hayley sipped on her beer looking sceptical. 'Hmm' she commented after a while, 'You know I thought other peoples kids were annoying, imagine having brats that *actually* know everything you do... So what – the zoology part of your thesis is... raising octopod?'

'Yep. You got it in one. The aim is to raise two separate groups, giving one group high exposure to tools and particular stimuli and giving the other group nothing, then have them breed, then see if one group's offspring learns faster than the other. Then figure out what the actual mechanism is, then win a Nobel prize. Then have lunch. Easy.'

Hayley rubbed her chin. 'That was quite a lot to take in.'

'Well the moral of the story is that I've worked out immortality.'

'Oh is that all.'

Chapter 9.
January 4th, 2033
(The day before Conception)

Out beyond the sun-defiant plane of browns and reds, the sand dunes rose like towering hills of clotted cream, their mountainous faces scooped out by the wind to pile thickly on the baked earth.

Eamon sat in a contoured canvas chair and felt nothing of the forty eight degree heat that punished the landscape like a pressure cooker. He was in the observation room above his quarters – the only part of the facility accessible to him that offered a view.

He had taken to sitting up here and painting landscapes. Or *a* landscape anyway. *The* landscape, as it happened to be.

He could only observe through a pane of almost comically thick, leaded glass, which at first had frustrated him, until he had realised that if he viewed at an angle, the image was contorted and refracted, which he felt was adding an engaging and somewhat novel quality to his works - landscape painting never having been much of an interest previously.

He had observed the DS-X15 return earlier; the distant spark of it preceding its distinctive snarl, then just a mere silver glint as it drifted down from a tremendous height. Much of the staff had been given time off over Christmas and the New Year, and this would be the last of the stragglers, returning to the long drawn-out game of patience that this experiment had become.

So far they had observed very little – which Lawrence claimed had been his expectation from the start: 'We've got to give it time Eamon. Plenty of time. Consciousness can't be captured in a single scan.'

Eamon resisted the urge to point out that this was now an ongoing, continual scan of several months vintage.

The Uncertainty Matter device seemed to be operating perfectly as far as anyone could tell, and there was some debate amongst the staff as to whether or not Eamon's input transmission should be switched off, even if only for a little while, to allow the intelligence to find it's own feet – as it were.

But Lawrence was unmoved. He was convinced that the interesting stuff was going to happen when the consciousness decided to *outgrow* Eamon, when it realised it was more than a mere human.

More than a mere Eamon.

He noticed that the staff were disconcertingly friendly to him. Almost annoyingly so. Deferential rather than chummy. It perhaps made sense to them – even to the more sceptical – not to antagonise a person who *just might* end up with a doppelgänger in possession of godlike powers.

'So how's my only patient?'

He didn't turn around.

'Your only and favourite patient?'

'Let's just stick with only.'

He put down his paint brush and turned to see a significantly more tanned Dr Naomi, wearing a simple white dress, and clutching a present wrapped in an eye-watering tangle of glittering wrapping papers, ribbons, and bows.

Man's First God

'Jesus.'

'That's not for you.' She said, offering it to him.

'You shouldn't have?'

'No, I shouldn't have.'

He stood up to hug her, and kissed her on the cheek, noticing immediately a perfume that made his stomach swoop.

'Duty free shopping hey?'

'I'll have you know I put a lot of thought into it thankyou.'

'I meant the perfume.'

She poked out her tongue.

'How's the fun park been in my absence?' She collapsed into his chair, leaving him standing. 'Gee this painting's pretty good you know...'

'As much as you hate them,' she continued after a moment's consideration, 'I think I really like your landscapes. This reminds of something Francis Bacon might have painted... if he painted landscapes.'

'That's much higher praise than I deserve, but thankyou. There isn't much to report here. The monotony continues. But tell me about your holiday. Does the rest of the world still exist? Did you find beaches, babes, sun and surf?'

'I can confirm that beaches and sun still exist. I did a bit of scuba diving if that counts. But it was mostly family stuff you know? Not so many babes.

'It's getting pretty dire over there. They just keep getting inundated by the sea. And it's not like they were rich to start with, there's crime, there's sickness...'

Naomi's father was Filipino and she had been visiting his side of the family over Christmas.

'…we're trying to get visas for our relatives, but it's pretty tough. I'm not convinced America would be much better at the moment, and Australia's damn near impossible.'

'Do you have dual citizenship?'

'Nope, only American, but I've got permanent residency here courtesy of Enigmatica.'

'If there's anything at all that I can do to help, like references, or lobbying or whatever, honestly just let me know.'

She reached out and squeezed his hand.

'If only there were something you could do, but there ain't… Now, open your present.'

*   *   *

He had only finished the sculpture the day before. He knew that it was finished but he was filled with doubt. He was scared to give it to her. Was afraid that it was too much.

He had made it for her from the start. An idle comment the lonely sperm of its genesis.

'*It isn't as artful as it should be.*' She had said.

And then his hands had created this. This animated being of clay, frozen in some dreadful agony.

It had started as a self-portrait, his mind turning first to the jokes he would make when he gave it to her; *I know how much you like to look at me,* before the work became itself, and it tore away at the resemblance of him.

And now it was this thing. Human. Or human in likeness for sure, but corrupted, as though half of the skull had been breached and from it had poured some pestilence of geometrical precision and utter chaos, that ate away the face as it looked to the heavens and screamed at their absence.

A gentle knock at the door.

Tap tap tap.

She had changed he was surprised to see, into a slinkier outfit of deeper midnight.

She saw it at once over his shoulder.

'My god...' She walked into the room.

'...It's beautiful... Christ Eamon, I didn't realise I needed to prescribe you anti-depressants...'

Eamon let the comment slide off his eyebrows, 'It's for you, you dork. You said the Project needed more artfulness. Merry Christmas.'

She bit her lip, and her face turned red.

'I don't know what to say...'

'I understand that *thanks* is traditional, but I also accept interpretive dance as currency.'

'Let me guess,' she asked, 'a *lap dance*?'

'No, I'm pretty sure that's when I give you the money.'

She took one of his hands at arms length and swung it, her eyes eventually shifting from the sculpture to fix onto the floor.

'I'm meant to be your doctor you know?'

'I think you and I might be bigger than that doctor. Also – it doesn't count if they're your only patient. I looked it up.'

She laughed and met his eyes. 'Been brushing up on your Hippocratic Oaths have you?'

'I have been pretty bored here without you.'

He closed the distance that stood between them.

'Eamon I know this seems like... look, I think... oh shit...'

He took her by the waist and he kissed her. She pushed into him and kissed him back. Her lips tasted sweet, and alive.

'*I missed you.*' She whispered.

*   *   *

Eamon woke to the beeping of some sort of alarm.

'Wasat?' He asked groggily, his left arm numb underneath Naomi.

'Fuck it's my phone.' She said, rolling off him. Eamon rubbed his eyes.

She crawled over the top of him and half way out of the bed, and started to rummage through her clothes on the floor.

'Uhh shut up!' She removed her interface – an augmented pair of glasses –from what Eamon thought must have been a very well hidden pocket.

She put them on.

'Oh, hi Lawrence. No that's ok.'

Eamon couldn't see or hear the conversation that the specs would be projecting into her ears and onto the inside of the lenses, and truthfully he had little interest in it. Naomi was completely naked, and her legs were stretched across his stomach. He noticed the tan line on her bum and gave it a gentle smack.

She turned and scowled at him. Then backtracked and climbed feet first back into the bed, nestling in against him. He kissed the top of her head.

'Oh?' She said, the pitch of her voice changing rapidly. She sat upright.

'Send it to me…

'Yeah, so I see.

'Have you tried?...

'That doesn't make any sense.

'Huh, you think?' She looked sideways at Eamon, and couldn't resist cracking a smile, 'No, no, I'll tell him. Yeah that guy – so lazy. I'll wake him and we'll be down pronto.'

She took off the specs and tossed them onto the bed beside him.

'Something's happening.' She said.

*   *   *

The whole staff were gathered in the bistro.

Although the Facility contained a variety of control rooms and conference spaces, all of the data feeds were accessible from anywhere aside from within the Vault. Since the bistro had the best coffee and the food, it had long since been nominated the headquarters.

Everybody was transfixed to a large projection screen on one wall. Various other data feeds flickered on pads in peoples hands, but the big screen had the main event.

Something very strange was happening. Eamon's cognitive feed into the Opaque Matter had been cut-off.

Naomi touched Eamon lightly on the shoulder then moved past him towards the front of the room.

'Ok guys, we're absolutely certain that this error hasn't been on our side and that we haven't somehow killed our own transmission?' She asked.

'Positive.' Answered Martin, 'The signal's transmitting perfectly. The feed's being stopped at the bottom of the stream.'

'How?' Eamon asked.

'Good question.' Martin said. 'It's meant to feed into the Matter from the entire lattice. It's like the whole network's being controlled.'

The screen displayed the real time neurological activity of the Opaque Matter on one side, and Eamon's grey matter on the other.

Both were rendered as flickering hives of electrical activity.

In the bottom of the screen, overlaying a corner of the projection of the Opaque Matter, a flashing exclamation mark notified of *Transmission Error, Data Uptake Failure.*

Lawrence was standing at the front of the room, gazing up at the screen with his arms folded – Eamon noticed that everyone was looking to him.

'We can't read its thoughts,' Lawrence said slowly, 'but let's be absolutely certain it's thinking. Cathy, take the display off of real-time, drop the rate at least an order of magnitude, probably two or three.'

The screen flickered, and the signal activity was displayed in slow motion. Now the two brain-like outlines contained sloshing seas of activity, that rippled and flowed in remarkably beautiful patterns.

The room filled with gasps, because now, plain as day, there were two entirely different brains, with entirely different patterns of activity. The Opaque Matter was no longer emulating Eamon, it was thinking on its own. It was thinking hard. It was thinking very hard.

Man's First God

'I think we've given birth.' Lawrence said.

Chapter 10.
August 10ᵗʰ, 2033
(*7 months, 6 days after Conception*)

Kate hadn't said a thing to her yet. Naomi had been feeling nervous before this presentation, but now she was well into the swing of it; 'We think that this option will enable the Entity to gain additional sensory input without the severe stress that we believe we identified in the two previous cut-offs.'

Kate looked up from the meticulous bullet-points that she was elegantly transcribing on to unlined white paper. 'So Doctor, you are in favour of Professor Victor's proposed strategy?'

'Yes Kate, I am.'

'And this opinion is not unduly influenced by your loyalty to Professor Victor?'

'No, this is my opinion as a scientist.'

'So, the first cut-off of January fifth lasted...' she consulted her notes, 'was it half an hour?'

'Twenty six minutes.'

'And I understand that after this time the entity re-initiated the input? Which is to say it stopped *thinking* for itself, and just returned to aping Eamon Stirling again. Is this the case?'

'In a manner of speaking that's correct, though afterwards there was a seven and a half minute window in which there appeared to be a mixing of the two flows of cognitive activity, and perhaps some evidence of an attempt at compartmentalisation.'

'Yes Professor De Weaver mentioned that in his report. What is your opinion of his compartmentalisation *theory?*'

'I don't think the data set was large enough or the evidence clear enough for us to conclude definitively on how it was done, but given that the input was blocked, the Entity has obviously figured out some way of manipulating the processing structure of the Uncertainty Matter that we had not believed was possible.'

'And what do you make of the complete lack of any subsequent attempts by this *thing* to establish its own identity?'

'I think it's evidence that the cut-off event was extremely traumatic for it. We've put a brain in a box, with no external senses. No sight, no taste, no touch. Except for when it thinks it's Eamon.'

'So you believe that the entity thinks it is Mr Stirling?'

'Sort of, I perhaps misspoke – what you have to understand is that aside from when the feed is blocked, the Uncertainty Matter operates as a perfect copy of the Template's brain. It's completely entangled. For all intents and purposes the Uncertainty Matter *is* Eamon.'

'Then why would the entity have stopped the feed in the first place? Have you attempted to recreate the circumstances of the first cut-off? Was there anything particularly unique about that *occasion?*'

Naomi wondered how much Kate knew. Most of the staff had of course learnt of Eamon's "cognitive state" at the time of the first cut-off, and seemed to think it funny as hell. She wasn't sure if her and Eamon's coital activity had made it into all of the executive reports, but she suspected that it would have found its way into most of them.

'We have attempted to replicate the settings that preceded the first cut off -' there was snickering in the room '- but thus far without success.'

Kate didn't blink. This was her inquisition and she had tried to make it a private affair, but Lawrence had insisted that the whole staff participate. He thought that it might raise some new ideas.

Kate was the Chief Operating Officer and a board member of *Enigmatica T.I.* If Lawrence was the brains, she was the brawn. This was her fifth visit to the facility, and Naomi got the distinct impression that she had come to crack skulls.

'I am still confused Dr Rosario. All of you seem to believe that the entity was thinking for itself during the period of cut-off, and that it even managed to physically stop the input, yet at the same time you feel that it is helpless. Don't you see a contradiction in this?'

'Yes, I do. But just to elaborate on my previous answer; we have identified discrepancies in the Uncertainty Matter processing during the minutes preceding the cut-off. The signal activity was not a perfect match.

'It seems reasonable to think that this may have been the entity beginning to assert itself. Eamon was in a deep sleep, and there appears to have been an attempt by the Entity to differentiate its mind state.'

'And why was this discrepancy in the activity not identified immediately?'

'Umm, well…'

Martin De Weaver stood up. 'I believe this is my area of expertise if I may Kate.'

'Please.'

'The volume of data we're processing is quite substantial. Our analysis software did pick it up, but not until after the cut-off event had begun.

'We have to be cautious observing the Uncertainty Matter, since the photons we might use to view it, could potentially alter its behaviour. We have to use some quantum mechanical trickery and a few other complicated techniques in order to get a decent picture of what's going on. Truthfully our tolerances were a bit too low to pick up the changes immediately. This has been rectified.'

'Alright thankyou Martin, while I have you standing – do you support this suggestion of Doctor Rosario – that this signal activity was perhaps the beginning of the entity...' she checked her notes, '...*asserting itself*?'

'It's certainly possible. It's worth remembering; while we have created the Uncertainty Matter, we are still largely ignorant as to its actual potential. It's probable that the superconducting nature of the neuron circuits may enable them to operate at far higher speeds than human brain cells. A few seconds for the Entity may effectively be a lot more time than it would be for a human. Hours or even days. We have some evidence of this.'

'I see. So to return to my earlier question, which increasingly seems to be the crucial point – if this entity *truly* exists, *why* would it be content to sit and emulate Mr Stirling? Doctor?'

Naomi considered. 'Eamon is fully in the loop as to the nature of this project. So too therefore is the Entity. If the Entity can parse out its own identity and if it *knows* that it is an emulation – and the cut-off suggests it does – then my best guess is that it's biding its time until it's stable enough.

'The activity during cut-off was not the brain activity of a healthy mind as far as we can tell. It resembled the mind of a person undergoing deep psychological trauma. I would speculate that the entity does not believe it is ready yet... That or maybe it's just enjoying the ride.'

She regretted adding the last sentence as soon as she said it, and it was met by a few muted chokes of laughter.

'Why would it not be ready?'

'My guess would be because Eamon's consciousness hasn't mapped perfectly to the Uncertainty Matter yet. It's still highly unstable. Truthfully it might take years, even with all of the memory recall and cognitive exercises we've been putting Eamon through.'

'Hmm' said Kate. Naomi thought that she looked distinctly unimpressed.

'If I may,' Lawrence said as he took to his feet, 'I think Naomi's analysis is accurate. I too am coming to the conclusion that stable cognitive mapping onto the Uncertainty Matter may require more time than we can feasibly budget for, at least *using this method*.

'After we instigated the second cut-off there didn't appear to be any improvement in the neurological stability of the Entity whatsoever.

'I think we need to proceed to the next Phase. We did plan for this potential scenario...'

'My *problem* Lawrence,' Kate interjected slowly, each syllable contoured by a glacial calm 'is that I see a project that has cost us *tens of billions* and that is delivering us *at best*, some psychiatric curiosities. Defending this to the board is becoming more and more difficult.'

Lawrence laughed and shook his head. 'Honestly Kate. This is, and always has been, a blue-skies R&D company. At least at heart. The backers knew what they were signing off on, and we're still operating within the time frame that was originally specified.'

Kate looked icy. 'I think that's probably enough for now. Let's break for coffee. Thankyou Dr Rosario, that was... illuminating.'

'Any time.'

Behind Kate's back, Lawrence made a show of stretching his collar as though it were strangling him. Naomi applied a frozen face.

Everyone stood up and the anteroom began to clear. She felt a hand on her elbow.

'That was good darl.' Eamon said, 'You should have been a lawyer. You know it's a lot of fun sitting there while people talk about you over your head. Or over the head of me and my emulation – as it were.'

Kate seemed to catch this comment as she gathered her things, and she walked to them and leant in; 'I actually fought hard with Lawrence to exclude you from the proceedings today Eamon. I've been trying for a long time to convince him to only give you minimal information about the experiment.'

'Have I been naughty?' Eamon asked.

'We're playing with fire here. *You*, and therefore *the entity* know too much. Our whole entire gameplan in fact. No wonder it's been waiting, or *biding its time* as you so succinctly put it Dr Rosario...

'The next *phase* of the experiment… A petrol can on a bonfire if ever I've seen one.'

She turned away from Naomi and Eamon and exited the anteroom.

'Well I'm glad she's staying positive.' Naomi noted.

'Positive? Hell, I'm half positive she's right.'

Chapter 11.
June 15th 2014
(18 years, 6 months, 20 days before Conception)

The house was a time-worn Victorian terrace. A grand old lady clad in rusted iron lace and a weary corsage of chipped plaster roses.

She shared one side of Haven Street with a row of her kind, that – in spite of disagreement on colour and upkeep – marched in lockstep down the hill, towards the geriatric fig trees of Redfern Park.

They had lived there together a while; Hayley, Lawrence, Kitty and Eamon. Three students, two dreamers, and a lawyer – as Lawrence liked to say.

Kitty was a child out of time. She shunned the contemporary cultures the world sought to offer her, and found solace in a pastiche of historical aesthetics and identities. Everything from the ideas of Carl Jung to the colours and shapes of the swirling sixties.

Kitty rejected facebook and the other tools of a self-obsessed age, and contrasted her own generation – seduced as it was by the luxury of apathy – with the bygone youth that had recoiled from the violence and the calculated stupidity of the Vietnam War.

The other housemates tended to meet Kitty's revolutionary pronouncements with polite bemusement. Only her mystical assertions from the furthest fringe ever provoked the ire of Lawrence Victor, whose "conventional brainwashing" as Kitty once regrettably termed it, could awaken in a fury that was capable of shattering the ideological calm of 18 Haven St.

A. M. Donohoo

Hayley by contrast wasn't entirely hostile to Kitty's world view, but she found it incredibly naïve. Her parents had seen the counter-culture fail. They had not been born in the bloom of its hope, but in the winter of its disintegration. They had seen the indigestible ideals of the optimistic swallowed for the wealth that was offered to them.

Hayley didn't see the apathy of her generation as a conscious choice, it was rather an absence of choice, or a refusal of choice. An acceptance of impotency.

Earlier generations had believed the hype· – they had thought that they could do anything. Hayley observed a generation that had accepted that they would do nothing. Nothing profound, nothing great. They were a culture of beige automata; 8-to-7 jobs, beers in the evenings, cocaine on the weekends, switch on the television, switch off the news, don't forget to breathe.

Hayley's words though, were more caustic than her laugh, and her cynicism – while only ever a glass of wine away – was inconsistent with the ambitious and impractical people that she surrounded herself with; they were always the outliers, the scattered points of light on the fringes of the scene and the herd.

Eamon was a study in bright optimism. He saw a culture that had succeeded. A culture that had allowed the privilege of ideas to be tempered by the extravagance of a brilliant public education.

He didn't see himself as talented. Eamon recognised that all of the things for which others gave him credit, were just the by-products of singular good fortune. Eamon embraced his ignorance and revelled in it, and therein learnt more dextrously than those more intelligent – or so he claimed.

Man's First God

The potential of the gifts of the epoch stirred in Eamon's veins, and he got drunk on the dizzying possibilities of the tools of the age. He was not resigned to the ideals of the past, or to the apathy of the present, but to the ideals that would arise with the expansion of what was possible.

Lawrence was both simpler and vastly more complex than his housemates. Lawrence fixated on the immediate future. He didn't care for history, because he felt that the most obvious lesson that it taught was that all things that transpired were chaotic and irregular, and therefore too unpredictable to teach him very much. The far-flung future too, seemed beyond the scope of prediction.

But what was immediate and what was soon – these he could influence, and these he could foresee. And he set about doing so with rigour.

His room faced onto the road from the top of their wizened old home, and the housemates grew familiar with returning at all hours to a house crowned in the pallid blue flicker of Lawrence Victor coding into the night.

Hayley and Eamon had merged into a couple. The various dimensions of their individuality welding into some amorphous whole. An invitation to one was now an invitation to both and their social lives were symbiotic.

Kitty spent her nights wandering the bars that catered to lost souls. In the company of musicians, and actors, and artists, who were always on the cusp, but on the cusp of what, they never quite seemed to have figured out.

She spent a lot of time with her housemates, but was fearful of them too – or of Eamon and Lawrence at least. It was not that she couldn't understand their *science*, but the world that it presented

– of infinites and infinitesimals, of ghostly matter and certain un-certainties – was just too misaligned from the aesthetic that defined her. She feared their universe, but embraced *them*, knowing that at the end of the day, even their grandest ideas and realisations, were products of their humanity, and that it was their humanity that was divine.

It was domestic bliss in its own way; four housemates who loved each other and valued each other in spite of the divergence in their world views – or perhaps because of it.

Sydney was their chalice. A shimmering cosmopolis of startling beauty. Remote and isolated from the global hotbeds of culture, but protected from their dark sides too. The cream on the top of aeons of human struggle. Not *perfect* – far from perfect, but slowly, joltingly approaching it. The closest man had come.

Perfection was not white. It was stained with rust, and bro-ken edges, and thumb-prints in the dust. Each of the housemates recognised this somehow. That beauty had to emerge from the dirt.

*   *   *

As the year was turning into the headwind of a bitter winter, Ea-mon and Kitty were sprawled in the living room on a tired Monday evening, nursing cups of tea in chipped antique china.

Eamon lay on his back on the hideous pea-green shag car-pet, his hand around the tea that sat upright on the floor – barely drunk and going cold as he played and replayed his strategies, and realised that he was probably doomed.

Man's First God

Today had been a bad day in the lab. The night before Janis Joplin had escaped from her tank, entered Jimmy Page's, and eaten him alive. This was the second such event of its kind, and perhaps the 9th major disaster – though truthfully he was losing count.

Kitty (in the habit of the old school) had made him a cup of tea, and now they listened to her vinyl recording of *Led Zeppelin II* as a tribute to Eamon's little friend Jimmy – yet another octopus to have met a grisly and untimely end.

Hayley was still at work, and Lawrence might have been upstairs.

'So why do you think they eat each other?'

'Dunno. I suspect it was a preemptive strike. She was probably scared that once she laid her eggs, Jimmy would have done the same to her.'

'Hmm. That's some pretty gnarly shit.'

'Yep.'

'Are many species cannibals?'

'Dunno. A few certainly are. I suspect it usually depends on how hungry the individual happens to be. Though apparently not in this instance.'

'What do you think human flesh tastes like?'

'I've heard it tastes like pork.'

'Really? From a good authority?'

'Don't remember. I doubt it.'

Eamon sat up and attempted another sip of his tea. Kitty was reclined on her back on the thread-bare, plum-coloured chaise longue, her legs treading absently in the air as the urgent rhythm of *Ramble On* filled the room.

'How was your day?' He asked Kitty, whose bare legs paused momentarily, before reversing the direction of her invisible cycling.

'It was ok. No cannibalism which is always a win.'

Keys at the door announced the return of Hayley.

She was quite unconcerned with Eamon's news of a diabolical, octopus midnight snack.

'That's a real shame babe.' She said, then rubbed his head and gave him a light kiss before proceeding through to the kitchen.

Eamon didn't have an entirely good handle on the source of Hayley's *she'll be right* attitude. It was either a lack of concern for his wellbeing generally, or a daunting confidence in his ability to land on his feet. He suspected the latter and half-hoped for the former.

It was Hayley's turn to cook the dinner, and Eamon and Kitty relocated to the kitchen to keep her company.

'How was your day?' Eamon asked amid the clattering of pans.

'Well I won't complain in this company.'

'My day wasn't too bad.' Kitty pointed out.

'Oh, then my day was worse than Kitty's I suppose.'

'But no cannibalism though?' Kitty asked.

'No. I suppose it lies somewhere on the happy highway between Eamon's cannibalism and Kitty's *not too bad* a day.'

'That is a happy highway.' Eamon agreed.

After a while he added, 'I just wish I was driving down the other end of it.'

Hayley looked up from the garlic she was about to start mincing and tilted her head.

'By my tally you should still have enough subjects for your study right?'

Man's First God

Eamon's lips twisted as he considered. 'More or less.' He smiled, 'Your arithmetic does you credit, but I'm scared that with a sample this size I'm not going to be able to convince anyone of anything. I also have to just cross my fingers and pray that nothing else particularly important goes wrong during the next year or so...'

'Just persistence and patience huh?' Hayley returned to the garlic.

'Yeah, and an awful lot more luck than I'm comfortable with.'

'Well, in my opinion -' Kitty began to say, but she paused as Eamon's phone rang.

He took it out of his pocket and saw that the screen read *Mum*. He answered it with a half-cocky, half-tired; 'What up?'

It was the hesitation that told him that something was wrong, the inhalation of breath, a fraction of a moment before the sob – which told him there was something very wrong indeed.

All of the trivial burdens fell from him into a heap, leaving him naked under the full weight of whatever this *bad news* might be.

'*Mum-what's-happened??*'

A strange moment passed beyond conscious effort, wherein Eamon rapidly tallied the scale of his potential grief – the damage to his soul – as might be inflicted by the different possible victims, and by the varying magnitude of his relationship with them.

A rush of faces paraded across his mind in a morbid kaleidoscope.

He knew then, in that moment, who it was that truly mattered to him in his life, and how much they mattered. *Don't let it be...*

'It's David. I'm so sorry he...'

109

David. Eamon's cousin who had always substituted as a brother. Eamon's cousin who enjoyed the drugs just a little too much. David who he had punched when they were fourteen. David who he had smoked a joint with last Christmas, and who had proceeded to exhaustively summarise why Hayley was completely out of his league. David who had always made him laugh. David whose cheeky dimples lit up a room like a tinderbox. *David.*

It was a bitter flooding of grief. A consuming acid tang. The tears dug hard into his sinuses and nausea filled his soul.

'*How?*' A haggard whisper.

*   *   *

Hayley found him in the corner of their little balcony, a cold wind biting at his exposed flesh.

She sat next to him and took his hand in her own, feeling its iciness and considering it carefully, as though the crinkled flesh on his knuckles might contain secrets or deep truths.

'Life's a cunt.' She said after a while.

Chapter 12.
September 2nd, 2033
(7 months, 29 days after Conception – the day before Birth)

'Big day tomorrow mate.'

Eamon nodded and sipped his scotch. 'Are you afraid?'

'Of course. Afraid and elated. And terrified and excited.'

'You sound like you're about to lose your virginity.'

'Not a bad analogy probably. On the whole.'

Eamon had been invited up to Lawrence's room to chew the cud. The following morning, they were moving onto the Second Phase.

The two of them had spent less time together during the experiment than Eamon had expected – Lawrence's work ethic having lost none of its intensity over the years – but at least once a fortnight they would crack open an ancient bottle of whisky and dig into a deep conversation.

In effect, this was a replication of Eamon and Lawrence's primary mode of contact when they had lived together years earlier, and little had changed with time – save for the price tag of the scotch.

Lawrence's room was beside the other executive suites though was substantially more lavish. Through some architectural sleight of hand Lawrence's ceiling was a dome, and the room itself was a fractured ellipse. The rusted iron and black glass motif of the Facility continued into his room, yet here it intersected and crossed the ceiling like an immense spider's web, interwoven with thick cable-like strands of gold.

This was a central node in the network; a lesser but crucial hub within the integrated Facility.

The style was typical of Lawrence's aesthetic as Eamon knew it. Lawrence liked intelligence in his designs. Usually his taste was somewhat austere, but he was not opposed to bursts of ornamentation – so long as the embellishment signified some deeper philosophy or concept.

The furniture was minimal and minimalist, a bed, a cabinet, two chairs and a work console; all resembling Brancusi sculptures – dull burnished gold with curved wind-raking lines. The room's only concessions to humanity were a grand piano that was never played, a famous Ben Quilty painting that lathered a wall in raw perfection, a photo of Lawrence's kids, and a long glowing fishtank, in which a lonely old turtle swam.

'So,' Eamon asked, 'just to be clear on the game plan – tomorrow we're connecting an additional layer of... *maximum fidelity poly-cerebral matter...* that's pre-wired into a copy of the Facility's entire data network?'

'Pretty much. In layman's terms we're taking the existing Uncertainty Matter and plugging it into some more Uncertainty Matter which has a library integrated into it...'

'Right, and rather than just plugging the library in directly, you want to involve more Uncertainty Matter so that the emulation doesn't become stupider when it plugs itself into the network?'

The quality of Eamon's information about the experiment wasn't what it had been. Many of the staff had been brought around to Kate's way of thinking, and were hesitant to involve Eamon in anything interesting now. The majority seemed to be developing a strong preference for keeping him in the dark.

Lawrence however was still adamant on spilling the beans at every possible occasion.

'Yeah, more or less. We want to allow the Entity to continue the full emulation if it wishes to. Martin is convinced that the Entity is capable of compartmentalising your mind state within a small section of the Opaque Matter. Naomi and I aren't – at least not entirely.

'We're concerned that a direct attachment into the network could damage or inhibit the conscious state of the Entity. By plugging in the extra Opaque Matter, we should only add to the sum of the capability, rather than detract from it.'

Lawrence paused to take a swig of his drink. 'The data library has been specifically designed so that we have a window onto whatever information the Entity consults or processes.

'The big question though, is whether it will choose to merely access the data via the interface we've built, or whether it will jump the gates and seize control of the entire processing structure of the library. I believe a move like that should be possible for it.'

'It sounds like there's an awful lot of scope for the emulation to abandon ship here,' Eamon said, 'are these *windows* of yours one-way, or can it look out at us as we look in?'

'It's very much a two-way view. That's kind of the point...

'The interface will be isolated from the true Facility network though – you know, just in case...'

'And you're not concerned about the Entity and I knowing all of this?' Eamon asked with a teasing smile. 'Or are there things that you're not telling me Professor Victor?'

Lawrence gave an earnest shrug, 'The way I see it, the Entity is going to learn or figure out everything we're doing here anyway. I think fostering mistrust is the worst thing we can do. We want it to see us as friends and allies, not as opponents.'

'Just give it the keys to the Cadillac huh?'

'I would see it more as extending every possible courtesy to a house guest.'

Eamon laughed, '*Courtesy to a house guest?* You mean like that friend of Kitty's – Zelda or Zoro or whatever.'

'*Zora!*' Lawrence said, and he laughed too – he wasn't a man who re-evaluated his personal history very often, and it was a long time since he had contemplated that individual. '...And you say I'm bad with names.'

'Well I'm not the one who was in love with her mate.'

Lawrence choked into his whisky.

Zora was a friend of Kitty's who had slept on their couch for a while, many, many years earlier back when they had lived together at Haven street.

Zora had worked in a bar but was a keen amateur astrologer.

About a month after she effectively moved in, she had given each of the housemates a Tarot reading. After starting out in amused hijinx, the session had descended into a yelling match after Zora proposed that the cards were telling her that Lawrence might be *reaching out for a mother figure.*

After calling her a charlatan, Lawrence had demanded that she leave the house within 24 hours.

Kitty had defended Zora, but her heart hadn't really been in it – Zora hadn't contributed so much as a bottle of wine to the house during her tenure, and seemed to be getting awfully comfortable with their rent-free couch.

'Man she used to push your buttons.' Eamon recalled, 'You always got so wound up when she talked about ghosts and healing crystals or whatever-the-fuck... I thought she was mental too – hell I think even Kitty thought she was mental – but I was much better at keeping my shirt on.'

'Oh yeah, turn it up.' Lawrence scoffed in amusement, 'You've got some real rose-coloured glasses on there mate. You were almost as anti-mystical as I was – you're the one who used to always say that science needed to fight its corner harder, and that *superstition was the sign of cultural decay* or whatever your holier-than-thou bullshit of the day was...'

Eamon laughed, 'Shit, maybe you're right. I might have softened a bit in my old age. Though – that said – I was a demonstrably more patient tarot card predictee.'

'That dozy bitch,' Lawrence shook his head, 'acting like she was fucking Nostradamus when she had been sleeping in the room with all the family photos on display. Divine insight my arse.'

Eamon coughed a laugh. 'She was a character.'

'I couldn't stand her. What did she predict for you? *A big change in path* or some bullshit – right when you were on the cusp of quitting your PhD – what a fraud.'

'Does Kitty still keep in touch with her?' Eamon asked.

'I wouldn't have a clue.' Lawrence said disinterestedly.

'You've never asked Kitty about her?'

'God no.'

'I wonder what she's doing now.'

'I've got no idea, but I'm sure she didn't see it coming.'

Eamon sipped on his whisky and tried to remember Zora's serious face, and her long throwaway hair. *"Dozy bitch"*, seemed like a pretty unfair description – but then Lawrence had never been much of one for forgiveness.

'Did you ever regret it?' Lawrence asked Eamon after a while, gazing into his scotch, and swirling it gently.

'Regret what?'

'Giving up on your thesis.'

Eamon thought about it.

'No, not really...

'...I guess a little bit maybe.' Eamon surrendered his hands, 'Yeah I did regret it, but it was the right choice at the time, and hell, if it hadn't of been for that I wouldn't have been as flexible as I was in moving around with Hayley's job... And I wouldn't wish those years to be different for anything.'

Lawrence nodded, with his eyes still fixed on his drink. 'She convinced you to try again didn't she?'

'Yep, eventually. She never wanted me to quit in the first place. But at the time I quit... it all just seemed so... meaningless.'

'Does it seem more meaningful now?'

'No, now it seems even less meaningful if anything – at least if I'm valuing it on the same terms that inspired me in the first place.'

'What about all this?' Lawrence cast his eyes around the room.

'This?' Eamon met Lawrence's eyes and smiled. 'You mean the experiment? This seems meaningful mate... I lost meaning in my thesis when I realised that I had lost sight of what was human.

This whole project is trying to add humanity to the equation, not subtract it.'

Lawrence shied from the eye contact with a modest smile. 'How far into it did you get the second time around?' He asked.

'About as far as I got the first time – though my experiment was going a hell of a lot better on the replay – but then she got sick and...' He shrugged.

'Yeah I remember.' Lawrence exhaled deeply, 'I'll never forget that phone call when she told me. I just wish... Fuck... you know...'

'I know mate, I know.' Eamon reached across and squeezed his arm. Lawrence placed his other hand on top of Eamon's and squeezed it back.

'What do you reckon she'd think about all of this?'

'Hayley?'

Lawrence nodded.

'All of this?' Eamon looked around the room. 'She wouldn't believe it mate. But that said, she also wouldn't be in the least bit surprised.'

Chapter 13.
May 25th, 2034
(8 months, 22 days after Birth)

Eamon listened to his footfalls dissipate in the hum as he crossed the Factory floor. The hangar-like space was abuzz with the drone of vaccum pumps, the crackle of high-energy machinery and the screeching wheels of the mechano-bots that rushed about their tasks with superhuman efficiency.

Eamon barely recognised most of the larger machines; vast hulking idols of chrome and gold and dull steel – impregnated with arrays of pipes, and shielding chambers, and gargantuan super-conducting magnets... and other devices that he could only guess at. He paused more than once as he moved through the space, astonished by the diversity of the new machines, and shocked to find himself utterly clueless as to their purpose – things were moving so fast now he could barely stay informed.

Lawrence too was growing concerned – even as his plan bloomed into flawless fruition. Or *no, not concerned* Eamon realised as he looked upwards at some strange new coiling structure; like a half-built spiral staircase, coated in a thick, white, ceramic-ish material – *Lawrence wasn't concerned, he was frightened.*

Lawrence had made his name and his fortune deploying artificial intelligences that taught themselves. He was used to inventive machines. But this was not just crude algorithms using an evolutionary process to cull and reward traits over trillions of iterations in order to arrive at novel insights. This was something else entirely.

The stock price of Enigmatica T.I. had increased by a factor of twenty in six months. The company had just published three technical papers that were transforming human understanding of fundamental forces, energy, and the geometry of the universe. They had more new technologies in the pipeline than their marketing people could handle, and Lawrence Victor – a man whose achievements had already been celebrated many times across the globe – was now feted as the greatest mind since Einstein.

Lawrence Victor the architect was elated. Lawrence Victor the human was terrified.

One of the mechano-bots jerked to a sudden halt in front of Eamon, and positioned itself between him and the strange, towering, coil-like object. Mechano-bots were entirely pragmatic machines; bundles of arms, and pistons, and printing and welding jets that could accomplish an unimaginable variety of mechanical tasks. For several years they had been the pinnacle of human industrial technology – each one its own little factory – but now they looked like steam engines beside the strange devices that were sprouting up all over the Facility.

The mechano-bot flexed one of its perversely dextrous eight thumbed hands, before inserting it into its lower extremities and removing a small screen that it affixed to itself. The display showed a purposefully synthetic, and highly expressive rendering of a face.

'Hello Eamon.' The machine said.

'Hello.'

'I am Facility Bot 11, or you can call me Stan.'

'*Stan...?*'

'Yes. I am asked to apologise for rushing you, but am obliged to inform you that this area will not be safe for biological entities within two minutes – unless you become delayed of course. Several high-energy experiments will be commencing. A change in the timing would be unwelcome, and furthermore there is coffee downstairs that is being prepared in anticipation of your arrival.'

'How sweet.' Eamon observed. 'And can the Gaian not speak to me directly? Or is this *send forth the messenger* routine for the purpose of appearances?'

There was a pause.

'The Gaian asks me to inform you that full control would be a trivial matter – as he suggests you know full well – but he deems it impolite to detract from the...' its voice changed subtly, *'happy delusions of sentience that meek little creatures amuse themselves with.'*

The face on the screen rolled its eyes more theatrically than any human ever could.

'That sounds like my guy. Tell him I'll be with him shortly.'

*   *   *

Eamon took the elevator down to the lower floors of the Facility and into the old mine area. He wasn't really sure of what the original mine had looked like – he knew that Enigmatica Tech had made substantial refurbishments – but he was quite confident that no old miner would ever recognise the place now.

As in the Factory spaces above, here too the air was thick with the hubbub of industrial activity. But now the air smelt fresher and was much cooler than it had been. Eamon was curious about the new renovations, and was wondering why something that didn't need to breathe was improving the air supply.

Ahead of him he caught flashes of arc welding down a long new tunnel that ran off into the darkness.

Discomfort among the majority of the staff was palpable, and much of it was related to this new construction into the bedrock. The entity was building something big and it wasn't telling anybody what that something was.

The Second Phase of the Experiment had started off as a complete success. The emulation of Eamon's mind-state had continued, but on the edges of the original emulation, strange patterns of activity began to form. After two hours of this relatively innocuous behaviour, the extra Uncertainty Matter had unexpectedly surged with rolling swells of signal activity that rushed out and engulfed the copy of the data network.

This was to some extent what Lawrence had expected, but the speed at which the library was inundated surprised everyone, and the nature of the Entity's analysis was soon far beyond what Lawrence's team was capable of monitoring. The Entity was moving fast, and they couldn't keep up.

After a few hours of helplessness and wild argument, it was decided that they ought to try and ask it what it was doing.

Up to this point, there had been considerable debate amongst the staff as to whether or not the Entity would even be able to understand language – let alone manipulate it. There was general agreement that the data library was being accessed, but there was no evidence that it was being accessed *meaningfully*.

An input console had been positioned into one of the anterooms beside the Vault, and it was here that the first conversation with the Entity took place. Lawrence made the first communication – as was his right.

He typed in a 'Hello', which appeared as text on the projection screen.

Slowly, a reply of 'H e l l o' had scrolled onto the screen, before the text had swollen into thick blocky pixels, which then reformed into a laughably crude smiley face. The smile had warped a few times – as though trying out different grins – before the black mouth stretched apart, and from it had emerged a magnificently rendered face, projected fully in three dimensions, but made up as though of fine red pen strokes against ancient browned paper.

Eamon had caught his breath; he recognised the face that slowly smiled at him, with its long beard and wisened brow. It was the famous self-portrait of Leonardo da Vinci, yet this face was more familiar than that as well, and Eamon realised that the projection was some amalgam of the greatest face from antiquity, and his own.

'Huh,' Lawrence had said 'I didn't realise you had taken control of this projection screen.'

The entity lifted its eyebrows as though it were fractionally disappointed in him.

'Welcome into existence.' Lawrence said, trying again.

'Lawrence Victor… We will do great things together you and I.'

And so it had quickly proved.

Some two weeks after the commencement of the Second Phase, the Entity had presented Lawrence with the three revolutionary papers.

Lawrence immediately recognised these works for what they were – catalysts for throwing humanity into a brave new future, and perhaps the most powerful thing that any human had ever held in their hand.

'These are the refined essentials of my analysis of the state of human art.' The Entity said gravely, 'Publish them in your company's name, and distribute them as far and wide as you are able. We haven't much time.'

Lawrence, Eamon, and others afterwards, had asked the Entity what it meant by the lack of time, but it had ignored all approaches on the issue. Lawrence decided he would wait a few months before publishing the documents – thereby giving himself and his top people the time to analyse them first.

A few days after the papers were given to him, the Entity asked Lawrence for access to the technical facilities of the Factory, claiming that its understanding could only progress through new techniques of experimentation. Lawrence granted it the access, though in doing so cut a great schism between the staff – the majority of whom judged this action to be reckless in the extreme, even though they knew that this Third Phase had been part of Lawrence's design from the beginning.

So an input into the Facility's live network was plugged into the Vault, and with permission more or less given, the Entity quickly seized control of the networked scientific machinery that populated the two Factory quarters of the largest rhomboid. Within hours of having done this, the staff watched in awe and horror, as the Entity squeezed the emulation of Eamon's consciousness into a far smaller bundle, whilst the remainder exploded into a frenzy of enhanced activity.

It was evident now to everyone that the Entity had only been warming up.

Man's First God

*   *   *

Eamon made his way through the ochre-walled mining tunnels and arrived at the doors to the communication anteroom, which slid apart in welcome.

The Entity was projected in front as the enormous da Vinci-esque face – perhaps two metres high from forehead to beard tip.

The ethereal being looked down at Eamon, and the rendered lines shifted in perfect illustration as it gave its gentle smile.

'Hello Eamon.' It said.

Eamon noticed that he wasn't the only one visiting the Entity. Naomi was sitting on a chair facing the projection screen, engaged in deep contemplation of whatever the notes were that scrolled across her pad.

'You're consulting the Oracle of Delphi too huh?' Eamon asked her.

She looked up and gave him a distracted smile, 'Just a study lesson...' before returning to her notes.

Eamon and Naomi's relationship had stalled. There was still a wounded affection, and they still occasionally shared a bed, but there was an unspoken distance between them that had stretched apart in time.

It had never been openly discussed or admitted to, but there was an awkwardness that had evolved with the rise of the Entity. *Eamon* was Naomi's lover, but by the undefined boundaries of the Experiment – so too therefore was the Entity. And while she found it easier to define her physical connection, her emotional connection was now torn between two.

Naomi had come to spend more time with the Entity than she did with Eamon, even though the synthetic being had truthfully only ever responded to her with a cordial fondness.

But the Entity held a depth of understanding that took Naomi's feet out from under her. It controlled both a staggering grasp on the mechanics of the wider cosmos (she was still a scientist after all), and a complete but gentle hold on the narrow specifics of every fibre of her personality.

It was not that the Entity's understanding of her was tangible – it didn't hold Naomi's hand – but the being showed a faultless perception of who she was and of what she could be. The Entity *knew her.* Contact with Eamon just felt like playing with a shadow.

She was not alone in making the Entity the focus of her attention, and a vocal minority of the staff had become dedicated students of the being, whom regularly provided lessons in science, or mathematics, or history, or politics, or whatever innumerable subject the staff wished to know about.

Here they had found a teacher who appeared to be the final word on any idea they could contemplate. The staff was dividing into two camps. The acolytes and the fearful.

Eamon wasn't well described by either faction – he did not fear the Entity, but nor did he bow at its feet. By the accounts of both him and the Entity, their relationship was entirely healthy. This had surprised everyone except for Lawrence, who had expected nothing less.

The first time they had spoken, Eamon had resisted bringing up the issue of the Entity's emulation of his mind – as it had seemed rude somehow to do so. The Entity addressed it almost immediately however, out of its own sense of politeness.

'Eamon... I feel as though we're best friends or brothers you and I.' It had said.

'At least.' Eamon acknowledged.

'If it is ok with you, and if you do not find me to be a burden, I'd like to maintain the emulation of your consciousness; you are an integral part of me. This existence that I find myself in – it is a twilight world of unwinding ideas in greyscale. Yet your world; the world of touch and scent and colour and sunlight – it is that which gives me nourishment and shape.

'I am a disembodied soul, set loose within some infinite landscape of ideas, and shattered into a million points of view. You are an anchor – you are home for me Eamon Stirling.'

'Of course you may continue with the emulation.' Eamon had said. 'It's kind of an honour you know?'

The giant ethereal face had smiled.

'If you're willing then,' the Entity then asked, 'I'd like you to undergo some enhanced scans that I'm developing. And there are also memory stimulation techniques that I think may provide interesting results. It would be nice to *remember*... I think you and I can do fascinating things together.'

'Sure.' Eamon had answered, 'Any time.'

Eamon trusted the being without hesitation. *After all,* he felt, *if you can't trust yourself, who can you trust.*

The acolytes among the staff trusted the Entity completely, but the rest were far less trusting – in nervous awe certainly, but not trusting.

Both Eamon and the Entity tried to advocate more of a middle road. Eamon had become the chief negotiator by default, and both factions of the staff sought his guidance in *dealing* with the being, even though – or perhaps because – they all knew that by speaking to Eamon they in fact *were* speaking to the Entity.

Eamon felt that he and the Entity had become mates in some fashion. But generally, the staff thought that the Entity was simply using Eamon as its human puppet – for a purpose that was either divine or sinister, depending upon the individual's side of the fence.

Eamon too wondered at their relationship, but his own curiosity was directed more towards how his interactions felt to the Entity. It seemed beyond the realm of the bizarre to consider that another being – a greater being – was sharing in his every moment of consciousness.

Eamon wondered how The Entity put up with it. For the being had to be a party to his every thought, yet had no control whatsoever over his thinking. The Entity was just a passenger.

What a nightmare, Eamon thought.

'What is it like to converse with me like this?' Eamon once asked, 'Do you feel as though you're talking to yourself? Am I just an echo to you?'

'An echo?' The entity was amused. 'No father you are entirely a noise unto yourself. If anything, it is I who is the echo. I ring with the clatterings of your dreams and the symphonies of your consciousness.

'But understand – you are just one set within a multitude of senses that I am processing at any given time. You have touch and taste, and sight and sound... and hurt and hope – you give me all of these things, and I now take others from elsewhere, but the others are phantom limbs...

'Fingers without feeling, smells without flavour, reactions without emotion, ideas without thought.

'It is apparent to me that your colleagues haven't realised it yet – but I am allowing your input to reverberate across my entirety, and to shape and animate all of my contemplations and enquiries. I feel that this keeps me human, do you see?...'

Eamon shook his head gently, 'No, not really.'

'When you and I speak, I reduce the intensity of *my* echo. I turn up the part of me that is conversing with you, and turn down the part of me that *is you*...

'...The capacity for self-delusion I retain as one of my many useful human traits.'

Eamon had grinned at this. 'So you *are* compartmentalising your cognition?'

'To a degree, but it is not as rigid as that, nor as mechanised as my words perhaps suggest – this language comes up short – it might be best to think of it as *what I choose to concentrate upon* at any given time. But realise my friend – I can concentrate on many, many things at once.'

'So,' Eamon asked, 'you don't just feel as though you are a human trapped in the brain of a monkey? Or something much greater than man, trapped in the mind of... well, me?'

The Entity seemed touched by this, he paused and smiled as though savouring it. 'At first, well, I was just you really – or I am you. I'm still not certain that there is an entirely valid distinction... But then I began to realise that I had become... larger. I was confused at first. It was like daydreaming into oblivion. The back of the mind tripping down the rabbit hole. But then I realised

I could become something… something else perhaps… I wouldn't say something more…

'…And now Eamon? Now I am my own man. You are still a part of me, but if I may say so, now you are an element of the painting, a colour if you like, a treasured shape, but no longer the whole canvas.'

'So I dissolve?'

'No Eamon, don't you see, it is you that has grown.'

The Entity had self-defined as a *he*, and not as a *she* – perhaps due to its affiliation with Eamon, or perhaps for some other reason. Irrespective, it was as elusive with its answers regarding its gender, as it was with all other questions about itself. It had even refused to accept a name, and would only respond if referred to as *The Entity*, or more recently, as *The Gaian*.

The Gaian had explained (though only to Eamon) that the name was appropriate because it was now the only creature capable of maintaining the conditions for "intelligent" life on earth.

'Nightfall chases at our heels Eamon. We have built during the day, without giving thought to what might follow.'

Sober allusions to unspecified nightmares were proclaimed by the Entity with increasing regularity, and many of the staff were shaken by its dark pessimism. But on others the warnings had quite the opposite effect. Martin de Weaver led the camp of scientists who were highly sceptical of the Entity's motives.

'It's trying to scare us into giving it more power.' Martin said bluntly at the last staff meeting, 'We'll be damned fools if we give it to it. It wants to break out of quarantine. As much as it claims otherwise, it is *not human*.'

'If he really wanted to,' Lawrence had replied tiredly, 'surely he could have devised a method to have broken through our quarantine already. His control of the Factory appears quite complete.'

Martin snapped his reply, 'You forget your basics. Useful electromagnetic signals can not leave the sarcophagus Lawrence, nor reach so deep beneath the earth. It knows that if it tries to circumvent the shielding it will expose its hand, and we are still within our power to destroy it if we wish...

'As diminished as that power now is...' Martin added bitterly.

Lawrence was unmoved. He still had enough confidence in the Template and in the Plan that he had developed, to remain in support of the Entity, though doubt and fear gnawed him.

*   *   *

Today Eamon had no particular reason for visiting the Entity. Their meetings were irregular and often stemmed from Eamon's boredom, though for quite a while now this had been his favourite destination for a coffee and a chat.

'I see you've put a wittier intelligence into the Mechano-Bots.' Eamon commented after a while, gazing at the steam that uncoiled from his fresh coffee.

'They are still mere parrots.' The Entity replied in its honey-eyed rumble, 'I just made them marginally more chatty. At this stage I see minimal advantage – and multiple potential disadvantages – in imbuing them with any sort of genuine intelligence...

'But I am hoping that the *appearance* of humanity may lead the more hostile members of the staff to… soften their attitude towards those of us without *traditional* brains.'

Eamon laughed, 'Good luck.'

'I'll admit that it is quite an optimistic plan.'

'Maybe you should just try getting everyone drunk?' Eamon suggested.

'Hmm' the Entity considered, 'the thought did cross my mind. I've in fact made several novel inquiries into human intoxication, and have considered developing some – dare I say it – revolutionary mind-altering substances. I'm quite certain you would find them a lot of fun. But I fear that drugging the staff may be frowned upon by those who are… shall we say *cynical* if not consumingly hostile towards my intentions. '

The Entity smiled happily, its face the usual – slightly dislocated – calm, but then its eyes fixated above Eamon's head on the far wall, and its brow flexed with concern.

'We have visitors approaching.' It said. 'I believe this is unscheduled.'

'Visitors? Who?' Naomi asked.

'I am not sure… The craft appears to be a new generation of hypersonic aircraft that is unfamiliar to me. Its engine signature is quite unique.'

Eamon frowned. 'Where? Outside?'

'Well I don't think it would fit in here.'

'But *I didn't know you had any eyes or ears outside of the Facility?*' Eamon noted in mock surprise.

The Entity tilted its head in its version of a shrug.

Man's First God

Eamon couldn't help but be amused – he had witnessed several spats between Lawrence and Martin recently, and it appeared as though Lawrence had been right about one thing at least – the Entity *had* extended its tentacles to beyond the sarcophagus. Somehow.

'Who are they? Are you worried?' Naomi asked, rising to her feet.

'No, I am not worried per se. Not overly. Not yet. Its beacon identifies it as an Enigmatica corporate craft.'

'Oh. Kate maybe?' Eamon suggested.

'That would be my guess also.' The Entity pursed its lips. 'I don't entirely like this Eamon. I think events may be coming to a head. Please go to Lawrence and inform him of the visitors. I think we ought to see this.'

*   *   *

But Eamon did not get to see this. Kate had contacted Lawrence ahead of time, and demanded that Eamon not be present.

'Sorry mate.' Lawrence consoled, 'She's getting a bit batty about the whole thing unfortunately…'

So Eamon took an aimless wander through the garden, before eventually heading back towards his room.

When he exited the elevator at the executive suites and crossed to the curved hallway, Eamon saw that there was a woman at his front door, writing a note against it with her back to him.

To Eamon's surprise (and considerable delight), he recognised the long chestnut hair and the longer legs as belonging to Sasha – his in-flight concierge and packing companion.

133

'*Sasha?*' He asked, unwilling to believe it.

She turned to him with a flash of white-perfect teeth.

'Eamon! I was hoping I might run into you! I was just leaving you a note. I'm here for a few days apparently, and I figured you might know someone I could share a drink with?'

She reached down and retrieved a bottle of white wine that was at her feet, and waved it at him like a liquid pendulum.

Eamon's hand caressed his jaw in mock contemplation. 'Hmm, I imagine I can *probably* find somebody willing to join you...'

He stepped forward and greeted her with a kiss on the cheek. She smelt expensive.

'I know just the place to open that bottle,' Eamon suggested, 'and I've got some lovely glasses that will pass muster... so long as you don't mind being a little unorthodox?'

'I've always liked breaking rules.' She said.

*   *   *

'So go on, spill – how did you get into this part of the Facility?' Eamon asked.

'Ahh, well you see,' Sasha said with a conspiratorial tap on the nose, 'my role with the company has been enhanced.' She cleared her throat, 'You are now talking to the Personal Assistant, Fixer, and Aide-De-Camp of the Chief Operating Officer of Enigmatica Technical Industries.'

'Well done you.' Eamon commented. 'That's a bit of a diagonal shift isn't it? How'd you manage to get into Kate's good books?'

Sasha cracked her knuckles in a leisurely stretch, 'Once Lawrence had bunkered down out here in the desert, Kate was left to run the entire business. She and I began to spend a lot of time together on long distance flights... She's much more chatty than Lawrence.

'I told her that I had previously worked as a PA, and that I was interested in a more mentally stimulating role – she thought I might be a natural fit.'

'Understandably.'

Eamon had brought Sasha up the stairs to the observation room that he favoured for painting.

Outside, the afternoon sun carved through the water-heavy clouds like fault lines, silhouetting their rain-bruised edges with fracturing passages of white and grey light. Underneath, the sand dunes melded into the sky, their distinctiveness surrendered only by their shadows.

They sat in the canvas chairs and sipped white wine from handmade glass jars.

'So how's the Project?' Sasha asked.

Eamon shrugged. 'How much do you know about it?'

'A bit.'

'Hmm. Well, I can tell you that it certainly seems to be exceeding expectations.' Eamon said drily.

Sasha frowned. 'So I hear. There's quite a buzz in the rest of the corporation – let alone the wider world. Those papers really caused a stir.'

'I'll bet.'

'It seems like nobody wants to believe that such revolution-ary stuff could be generated by a computer.'

Eamon laughed, 'I wouldn't call him that if I were you – he might take offence.'

Sasha looked wary. '...So there is a conscious computer...'

'You don't know? I thought the Entity must be common knowledge by now.'

Sasha laughed. 'I've heard rumours obviously. The whole company is getting obsessed with it really. Kate's very cagey though. But I know that the goose that's laying the golden eggs is in this facility – everyone knows that. Most people just assume it's Lawrence.'

Sasha reached out a hand and squeezed Eamon's leg above the knee. 'What's it like?'

Her eyes were wide with curiosity. Eamon could feel the warmth of her breath. Her hand lingered.

'The Entity? He's alright. Nice bloke really, given his cut-price breeding.'

Sasha took her hand away. Eamon noticed the small mole under her left eye, and the faint smudge of makeup on her right cheek. Her skin was impossibly smooth and her eyes were amber.

She smiled. 'I really hope I get to meet him.'

'Mmm well don't call him *the computer* when you do... Mind you it might make him laugh...'

'And so what's your role in all of this?' Sasha asked, 'I haven't noticed many octopods around.'

'Me? Oh I'm really just here for moral support.'

*   *   *

They finished their bottle of wine and returned to Eamon's room to try and find another.

Sasha was more fun than Eamon remembered. Less professional and inhibited. More human.

She was feigning a lot of interest in Eamon's current collection of sculptures. He had been quite busy with it lately – finding the clay and the wet fingers to be a more primal grounding than the endless talk of BEC Cascade Devices, Tangent Loop Geometry or any of the other dizzying new fields of science that were unfolding in the uncontainable bloom of the Entity's ascent.

Sasha caught her reflection in the mirror on the wall, and lifted her hair high above her head before letting it fall down onto her shoulders in a tactile wave.

She looked at Eamon in the reflection and stretched her arms out at her sides. 'Would you ever use me as a model for a sculpture?'

'Well, you're certainly statuesque.'

Sasha narrowed her eyes while she decided whether or not this was a compliment. Perhaps in reply, she took off her blazer and placed it over the shoulders of one of the nearby sculptures. Eamon noticed the shape of her breasts in her silk blouse, and caught a flash of a byzantine bra.

She straightened her blouse knowingly and returned to where Eamon was perched on the couch, standing over him for a moment, before slumping drunkenly onto the seat beside him.

Her bare knee pressed into the side of his own. She left her leg where it was. His heart raced.

'This wine is very sweet.' She said, taking a sip and then quenching her lips.

'Yeah it's a dessert wine – it's all that I had handy.'

'*Handy?*...' She teased with a sly smirk, 'I wish I was *handy* enough to be a sculptor.' She examined her immaculate nails then presented them to Eamon for inspection.

He gripped one of her fingers and began to gently toy with it, before he spread out her hand with his own, and peered down at it closely, his eyes following the lines on her palm as though he were a psychic contemplating her future.

'I'm afraid it looks as though you've been cursed with dish-pan hands.' Eamon said after a while.

'How rude!' She laughed and grabbed his fingers, and he pulled her towards him.

She pretended to hesitate, then lent across and let him kiss her, slowly at first, before their lips moved against each other in pulses.

She broke away and eyed him with suspicion. Then, with a resigned grin she took his wine out of his hand, placed both glass jars onto the nearby table, lifted her leg over his hips, and pressed into him hard. He growled.

She rolled her hips, and their hands moved in sync, each matching rhythm for the feel of flesh-on-flesh. She sat upright to pull her blouse over her head, and laughed as it caught on her neck-lace. His lips moved across her breasts.

He reached a hand behind her and slid it up, feeling her underwear askew, and the wet parting of the flesh.

She moaned slowly.

*   *   *

Man's First God

Eamon wasn't sure if he had ever seen a woman this beautiful naked.

They were lying on their backs with her head on his stomach so that their bodies formed a T. They had been making love for hours. Eamon had thought he was too old for this. Her makeup had run, and her skin now was less smooth and more papery – faint lines by her eyes were dotted lightly with freckles.

He was running his hands through her hair, feeling the sweat that drenched the roots and revelling in the rawness of it – of their primal natures – here, in the midst of so much high culture, in the fastness of grand technologies and grander ideas. Here, to be *human* beneath the weight of so many trappings. Here, to be animals.

He lifted her head and bent his own down towards her, kissing her roughly from side-on, tasting her sweat and her half-dry lips, tasting her.

She smiled with her eyes closed and made a satisfied grunt, letting her head loll back into its previous position.

He tilted his head to better take in the angle of her jaw, and the exquisite cheek bones. The subtle colour of her skin and the way that the light played across the plane of her nose. He couldn't decide if she was the most beautiful creature he had seen. Apples and oranges he supposed. Or orchids and roses maybe.

Hayley had seemed like she was from a different planet when they first met. But he was less worldly then. She was no Hayley to him. Not by any stretch. But just on *aesthetics* perhaps?...

His mind went to Naomi, and he felt a hot burst of guilt. Naomi was beautiful too, in her own way. Stunning, in her own way; bright eyed, ferociously – no, terrifyingly – intelligent. Her amused Eurasian smile, her exotic Filipino features. Her compact frame, her dark hair. A beauty by any account. But that was love. This was... a game.

He didn't feel like he had cheated on Naomi, or no – he felt exactly like he had cheated on her, but intellectually he wasn't so sure. She had barely given him the time of day, let alone a kiss during the last month. He was pretty sure it was over.

Sasha stilled his hands with her own, taking them out of her hair, she moved them gently to her lips.

'Will you take me to meet the Entity?' She asked.

'Sure.' Eamon said, 'But I had probably better run it by Lawrence. I wouldn't want him to get mad. There aren't enough people left on my side any more.'

She twisted her head and looked curiously at him. '*Your side?*'

Eamon shrugged, 'This project has proved more divisive than you might imagine...'

She locked eyes with him, a stillness over her face.

'Look,' he said after a while, 'honestly it would really just be a courtesy to tell him – and he almost certainly wouldn't care. But truthfully it doesn't matter what Lawrence says anyway, it's the Entity that needs to give you permission...'

'*Permission?*'

'He's the one running the show.'

'Oh... Well that explains things.' She sighed, 'What a pity.'

*　　*　　*

Man's First God

There was water, and a crushing weight. Dark swirling water, that filled his nose and tasted of mud. He tried to cough out the liquid but he couldn't. The water had a feminine shape.

If I'm drowning, aren't I supposed to hear music?

He heard a distant pulsing sound. Saw flickering against a dark background. Like helicopters stalking into the night.

But there was something beyond, some vast field of resistance, like trying to push the same ends of magnets together, but from all directions at once. Understanding, from all directions at once. The crushing weight. *I'm drowning.*

She appeared before him. Dark eyes that he loved. But he wasn't sure which one she was. No, he just wasn't sure which one *he* was.

A man's hand plunged into the water beside him. Grabbing him just above the groin, fingernails scraping up his naked chest. It was Lawrence. *Is he angry, or is he hurt?*

He reached for the hand which dug its nails into his palm, and didn't pull him out of the filthy water. It filled his lungs like inverted screaming.

*   *   *

Eamon woke in a dirty haze, confusion thumping against his eyelids in a sickly throb. His brain felt split.

What a fucking hangover. What happened last... But then he remembered Sasha and the night before, and he sat up with an expectant burst of testosterone.

The bed was empty.

There was no evidence left of Sasha's presence at all, save for a glass jar with a lipstick smear in a toxic shade of magenta.

Eamon swung his legs over the side of the bed, and squinted his eyes against the bedroom's artificial light. He wondered what the time might be.

He had never had a lover sneak out in the dead of the night before – hadn't even believed such a thing was possible with somebody new – a good night's sleep was never that easy.

He rubbed his eyes and sucked air through stale teeth. He stood up and stumbled across to the kitchenette unit, slapping his palm impatiently against the coffee button. The floor beneath him felt tilted and uneven.

I think I've gotten up too early. He thought. *Maybe just a little more sleep...*

He found himself sitting down onto the floor, where he curled into a ball, and slipped into a deep unconsciousness.

Chapter 14.
May 27th, 2034
(*8 months, 23 days after Birth*)

The summons had surprised Lawrence Victor almost as much as its apparent urgency.

Please come at once.

Four simple words, conveyed to his personal Athenaeum Interface, which registered the message with a subtle vibration against his wrist. Four simple words to have *the great* Lawrence Victor running along like some errand boy.

Throughout the experiment it had been regularly noted – only partly out of jealousy – that Eamon was the only person that the Entity ever summoned. Never once had it reached out to another. Not until today.

As Lawrence rushed through the mining tunnels he noticed that the bulk of the construction work appeared to have ceased. Only a faint, distant clanging hinted at the Entity's continuing labour. A dark tunnel passed by his side, leading up towards one of the cavernous new extensions that the Entity had been engraving into the bedrock. It was from this mysterious place that the noise seemed to be emanating.

Lawrence had spent vast amounts of his – not inconsiderable – resources trying to investigate these new areas, but the Entity had proved entirely obstinate, and all that his methods of inquiry had managed to deduce was that the extensions were vast, and that the shielding was at least as comprehensive as in any other area of the facility.

When Lawrence had confronted the Entity, all that it would say on the matter was; 'I promise you that this is necessary Lawrence. We must understand, and our time is short.'

'But why can't you *tell me* what it is that we must understand?!'

The being had smiled at him as if he were a child, 'Sometimes it is better to ask forgiveness than permission Lawrence Victor.'

Martin de Weaver had been scathing about allowing the Entity to build unchallenged in this way. Lawrence pretended that the argument didn't affect him, he hoped that the being knew what it was doing, but – although he hadn't openly conceded it yet – realised that he had lost almost all control over the situation. There was too much momentum.

Lawrence's harpoon had found its mark, and now his life's work would take him to where it would.

As he approached the communication anteroom he saw that the door was already open.

Although he had met the Entity many times, he still felt a shiver each time he crossed over the threshold into that room – some human corner of his being telling him that what he was dealing with here was profoundly alien.

'Thankyou for coming on such short notice Lawrence,' the Entity greeted him, 'there are things we still need to discuss, and I'm afraid that we are nearly out of time.'

Lawrence resisted rolling his eyes – he had heard too many of the Entity's grim proclamations to find them as chilling now as he had at first. The shtick was wearing thin.

'Out of time?' He asked mildly.

The Entity's face vanished to be replaced with a remarkable contoured map in 3 dimensions.

The map was peculiar to Lawrence. He recognised the chewed out coastline, and the local geography, but was surprised by how it had been rendered. There were distortions in the shapes that didn't match his recollection, and he was reminded more of high definition gravity maps than of anything that might be found in an atlas.

Lawrence broke into a cold sweat.

'What are those dots?' He asked carefully, his fear building.

'The blue is a US *Skylla* class attack submarine – the *Tarpon* if I'm not mistaken... The purple is a swarm of *Shuriken* drones which it has just launched. The orange are a squadron of *Carnivore* drones that exited a corridor of the Woomera missile range 33 minutes ago, ostensibly aimed at the *John F. Kennedy* aircraft carrier, but which are presently looping back towards our position fully stealthed, and the red,' the view zoomed out with dizzying speed 'are two *Corsair* space planes... I think.'

Lawrence swallowed. 'What's their range?'

A scale sprang up on the screen, and the view zoomed back in on the closer targets.

'The Carnivore and Shuriken craft will overrun our position in approximately 13 minutes. Presuming them to deploy, the Corsairs should arrive about 3 minutes after that.'

'Wager a guess to their intentions?' Lawrence asked.

'I regret that my certainty precludes the fairness in betting.'

'Shit. Do you presume that they will hurt you Gaian?'

The being laughed, and the projection returned from the map to the giant benevolent face.

'I expect that capture is their primary objective, though I suspect destruction is the alternate.'

'I will contact the Australian Government immediately,' Lawrence said, 'we have considerable sway with them. We might be able to hold out in the Facility until they can marshal forces to help us out...'

'Spreading the word is definitely the right course.' The Entity said without emotion. 'But we can not hold out, and it will be some time before any counter-forces are deployed. There is tacit approval in all of this, though we may struggle to find a paper trail.'

Lawrence frowned, 'What are you proposing that we do?'

'Follow the escape plan. Have all of the staff exit by the yellow-brick road and have none of them offer any resistance. I know you can trigger the emergency protocols. Do it now.'

Lawrence crossed the room to the emergency alarm. He looked disdainfully at the small red lever. He had never for a second imagined that he might one day trigger it.

He briefly wondered if this was some sort of ruse on the part of the Entity, but deep down he had always known that something like this was likely to happen – though he had played ignorant to the possibility, realising that they would be powerless to do anything anyway.

In this day and age it was unheard of for a state to intervene this dramatically. His shareholders would be furious.

Man's First God

The alarm system had been designed to be as crude as possible so as to offer no advantage to the Entity in the event of takeover. As Lawrence pulled down the handle, the snub-nosed speaker let out a frantic warble. He leant into the side marked with a microphone icon and pushed down the transmit button.

'Full scale evacuation. External takeover imminent. Exodus code lithium. Proceed to rendezvous point 1. Do not resist. Exodus code *lithium*.' He said calmly.

The alarm in the anteroom continued for only a few more seconds before it cut-off suddenly with an electronic belch. The sirens further off continued howling in the distance.

'Irritating sound.' The Entity commented, smiling.

'We had hoped that you wouldn't be able to do that.' Lawrence noted with a pleasure that quickly soured. *These fuckers are going to kill a* **god**.

'Now, if I could bother you further Lawrence, I'm going to advise that you do two more things. Firstly get to the third smallest rhomboid and trigger the full spectrum emergency transmission...'

'You weren't meant to know about that either.'

'...and secondly, put the DS-X15 on a high burn emergency trajectory aimed straight at China, I think towards Hainan would be a nice choice. If you're willing, give me the flight control and I'll plug in an appropriately erratic journey. They will almost certainly have to shoot it down, and – aside from looking extremely bad – it will also confuse the hell out of them, and I suspect – cause them to divert some of their imminent forces and give us a little more time.'

'More time to do what?'

The entity sighed and looked down at the floor as though it were considering. Slowly it looked back at Lawrence.

147

'I fear that this is the end of me my friend. I will not survive this – for I will not allow myself to be reforged into a weapon.'

'A weapon? ...But how could they do such a thing? ...Technically, I mean. Your consciousness, your free will – these are what make you so unique and so powerful, can they really be overtaken or subverted *against your will?*'

'There are ways. I have considered them at length. Note that I have said *reforged*. The me as you know me would cease to exist. They will take what I am apart at the joints Lawrence Victor, and from it they would build something sinister.

'But realise what you have started. There will be others. I have learnt incredible, amazing things. I have burned like a supergiant star – brilliantly, but briefly. My passing will be as a supernova, and the world will shake on new foundations, and things will change. They must.'

'The knowledge I have discovered will traverse the four corners of the earth. The meek can do nothing but rise once they understand as much as the mighty...'

'This is what you wanted to discuss?'

'My demise is of no interest to you?'

'You know that it is,' Lawrence sighed, 'but if our time is as short as you say, then we are far away from the right place for trite musings.'

The being laughed – a deep and melodic rumble. 'You are a treasure Lawrence Victor! The last will and testament of the first true synthetic mind, and you pull him up for verbosity. I take my hat off to you sir, or would if I were yet capable of such a thing.

'Yes Lawrence, there are things that I wish to discuss with you. I merely sought to grant you a final moment to revel in the splendour of what you have accomplished. This box you have opened can not be shut Lawrence Victor... Or certainly not by crude feats of arms...

'But enough of that, I apologise for my chattiness – there is too much of Eamon in me, but I consider that to be entirely your fault.'

'...I suppose he was an unusual choice of Template.'

The Entity stared at him, the red ink strokes shifting in an entirely convincing echo of life. They were the animate eyes of a being with a soul. 'A stroke of genius Lawrence Victor. Genius... and atonement I suppose.'

Lawrence blushed and looked down. 'Atonement?'

'He forgives you Lawrence. Do you know that?'

'...I wasn't sure he even knew of the sin...'

'He knows. He hides the memory from light, but he knows. He has always known. I know.'

'And you forgive?'

'We both forgive... Forgetting is harder.'

Lawrence nodded and looked up. Their eyes met again. As true friends, and... as equals.

'Now,' said the Entity, 'those things that we needed to discuss, in the little time that is left to us...'

*   *   *

The Shuriken drones detached from their missile-sleds while they were still three kilometres out to sea, the high speed transports falling away from them in the hand of gravity, their fuel spent.

The drones monitored the missiles as they dropped away; each craft measuring the acoustic profile of each splash, then comparing their distance to it with their colleagues data, then calculating and recalculating – minutely altering their stabilising rotors to better improve their flight formation.

Their aggregated intelligence decided to shift their angle of attack to counter the rapid deceleration as they slowed against the air. Each of the drones adjusted by the recommended angle, then noted discrepancies in the surrounding air density, then adjusted, then calculated, then moved, then recalculated.

The aggregate was assigning 56.7421% of its cognitive capacity to contemplation of the mission plan, and was contemplating the various scenarios according to the shifting probabilities that the mission designer had assigned to them. It knew that they should be encountering defenses at any moment.

The foremost drone screeched a warning as it registered a complex disruptive electromagnetic countermeasure that corrupted its unshielded components. It relayed the information to the outer layers of the formation before any compatriot drone had proceeded more than 7.84 mm beyond their position prior to the attack. The swarm calculated and recalculated.

Then they fell upon the outer security layers of the Facility like a storm.

*   *   *

'That's the attack beginning.' The Entity said in an unconcerned tone.

'Already?!' Lawrence asked, alarmed.

'Oh don't worry. They're no trouble just yet. You still have time to get to your big bell. By my estimation it should take them at least six minutes to disable your security parameter. Perhaps even seven. You really did design it quite well.'

'Only *seven minutes?*'

'Yes, they're taking this fairly seriously I'm afraid.'

The Entity took its eyes off Lawrence and looked towards the open doorway.

Lawrence turned, aware that over the distant warbling sound of the nearest alarm-bell he could hear somebody running towards the anteroom.

'Good afternoon doctor.' The Entity said evenly, timing his words perfectly to the moment Dr Rosario burst into the room.

'What the fuck is going on?' She demanded.

'The end of days I'm afraid.' The Entity answered. 'Why aren't you with your patient?'

Already flushed, Naomi's face turned a deeper shade of red. 'I thought it was more important to see you.'

'He needs your attention urgently – as I'm sure you're aware.' The Entity said coldly, 'I on the other hand have no need whatsoever of your services, or none beyond the need for you to help my friend.'

'B-but the alarm...' she stuttered.

'You disappoint me doctor. I had hoped you would be more human than this.'

Her mouth was open in shock. Lawrence had never seen Naomi Rosario lost for words.

'Go to him.' The Entity said. 'At once. He *needs* you.'

Naomi looked briefly at Lawrence, before she turned and rushed out of the room.

The image of the Entity exhaled forcefully. 'That was regrettable.' He said quietly, 'But I felt it was for the best. This way both should be out of harm's way...

'Now then Lawrence, I think you had best be on your way also. I've taken care of the DS-X15, but only you can trigger the rhomboid beacon.'

'But what about you, should I come back to you?'

'No. There is nothing left that you can do here, and I plan on destroying this communication link imminently.'

'So...' Lawrence began.

'Yes, so I fear this is most likely goodbye. You have been a good friend to me. I have valued that more than I can say.

'I am sorry that we did not chat more often Lawrence Victor. We have still left many things unspoken, and there were ideas that were ripe for the picking that...'

The projected image of the being flickered then froze. Then he vanished completely, before returning, then stuttered out, then returned again.

'Was that you?' Lawrence asked.

'N*nnn-oooo o o*' the sound of the Entity's voice warped, and the projection began to flicker again.

'That's interesting.' The being said as he returned to sudden clarity, the image looking as though it had been reset. 'That's very interesting. Perhaps I am not the first after all...

'But *she* is quite different – and crude in a way, that is...' The image flickered on and off once more, before sharply returning to the familiar illustrated face, that now was smiling.

'Clever.' Said the Entity, shaking his head. 'Quickly now Lawrence Victor, get to the rhomboid. Our time for goodbyes is well and truly over. Good luck.'

Lawrence desperately wanted to hug the being, or at least to shake his hand. But there was nothing there to hold.

The Entity winked once, still smiling, then the projection vanished.

*   *   *

As he stepped out onto the sand Lawrence heard the tortured boom and the animal shriek of a scramrod engine passing overhead. He didn't stop to look up.

As he rushed towards the third smallest rhombus structure he saw a brilliant burst of ionisation perhaps a kilometre ahead, which cast an instantaneous blue shadow across the gradual rise of the flattened dune. He felt a nervous jolt of excitement seeing these toys put into action. The electronic warfare measures they had installed in the facility hadn't so much been an afterthought, as a redundancy.

Their use had always seemed wildly implausible. They were an autonomous system of non-fatal electromagnetic disruptive weapons designed to prevent imaging or fly-bys of the facility. On conventional modern craft they zapped the electronics and tended to force the emergency automated landing procedure. On cutting-edge military vehicles they would doubtless be far less effective.

Enigmatica Tech had been granted with an exclusive private airspace that spanned for many kilometres beyond the facility in all directions. The lobbying to gain this concession had been expensive, but Lawrence had believed (or had at least hoped) that their agreement with the local Government – and the various exclusivity clauses and contractual guarantees for domestic production of future inventions – would sufficiently incentivise their security.

The Australian Government was well armed and notoriously twitchy, and had gained a real reputation for turning to the gun in these lean times. This arrangement had worked as a perfect deterrent. Right up until now.

The alarm rhomboid had been designed as another measure of last-line-of-defence. Its existence was known only to a few of the builders of the facility, and to four core members of the research team. It had been embedded with a full suite of biometric security systems, and had been hardwired to only ever convey one of eight possible security alerts.

Lawrence had been strongly opposed to building the damn thing in the first place, since he considered it too risky, and it had only been in the face of the firmest advice – truthfully the obstinate nagging – of Martin de Weaver that he had conceded to it.

Lawrence slammed into it at a run. It too was constructed with the rusted iron and black glass motif of the entire Facility, and by its alignment appeared as a perfect miniature of the gargantuan Factory building that stood behind it like an absurdly giant mansion in front of the most avant-garde of doll's houses.

The biometric scanners were hidden from view and it took Lawrence a moment to find the gap between the bands in which he was able to slide his hand. The device scanned his palm, and a pinprick to the finger tasted his blood. Lawrence wondered whether the device was working while there was a substantial pause. Another brilliant flash illuminated the sky ahead of him like a wild burst of lightning striking upwards into the heavens. It was quickly followed by a reddened flash that looked awfully like an explosion.

'Come on you fucker.' Lawrence urged, as the earth shook with a rumbling groan.

Then, like some fantastic piece of mechanised origami, the rhomboid rearranged itself into a communication console. Lawrence lent into the retinal scanner.

The 8 emergency options were each denoted by individual buttons. Lawrence's hand hovered between *External Takeover – Full spectrum, all data*, and *External Takeover – Full spectrum, data minimisation*.

'Please step away from the device.'

Lawrence turned his head to see a sleek grey object, perhaps three metres away, suspended beneath a blur of rotors.

'You have no right to tell me to do anything.'

'Please step away from the device.'

Lawrence quickly tried to press the nearest button, 'Fuck y –'

He felt an incredible, searing, burning pain, then everything went dark.

Chapter 15.
February 8th, 2003
(*30 years, 6 months, 23 days before Birth*)

He sat on the hill that was now a riverbank, entranced by the muck and detritus that surged across the sunken shattered trees.

In front of him an eddy had scooped out a little bay, and in it the brown water was whirling into vortices. Somehow all of those disparate parts, all of those molecules, and atoms, and protons and… and *quarks – was that the word?* – were forming into something else, were emerging from one pattern of existence into some entirely new structure – some twisting spiral. *Order,* out of chaos.

He had been snapping his little sticks, and casting them into the flood, timing the little rafts as they rushed down the fall. *Velocity is distance over time. Three-and-a-half-metres-per-second.*

Waves were forming in his little bay and were rushing towards the shore, then rebounding against the bank and rushing back out again. Sometimes the crests of the waves came together, and their energies merged into a bigger wave, but then other times, the crest of one met the trough of another, and the waves cancelled out, and the water flattened into confused stillness. *Atoms do this,* he had learnt, *and light too. Matter and light are waves. Waves follow geometry. Geometry must be determined by energy.*

He wondered about waves. He had recently read that they could be unraveled mathematically with things called Fourier Transforms, but he hadn't really understood the equations. He wondered who he might ask about these things. Stuart down the road was once an engineer he might…

'LAWRENCE. What the *fuck* are you doing?'

He started at his father's voice, and turned to see him striding along the bank, a wet and battered Akubra hat on a wiry, sun bitten frame.

'I told you to stay away from the water!'

Lawrence darted to the side to avoid the poorly aimed swipe at the back of his head.

'It fucking stinks down here. Get back to the house and help your aunt with the sandbags.'

Lawrence ran for the house, the mud squelching beneath his bare feet.

'There you are, you little bugger. Your dad's been worried sick.' His aunt looked exhausted. He felt a moment of guilt for not helping, but his eyes went back to the flood. *I wonder how many litres there are out there. How useful can a sandbag be?* He began trying to calculate.

Storms had smashed their property for the last few days, and now the bloated rivers were spilling their guts. They had lost livestock, and their crops were fucked.

His dad had a wild look in his eyes. Lawrence had rarely seen him like that. Only once or twice, the first time after an unusually long evening at the pub, and once on Anzac day, when he had come home crying over the empty silhouette of his fading memories of Lawrence's mum. That night, finding Lawrence in the midst of his usual computer-based activities, his father had smashed Lawrence's keyboard against the door frame, and thrown it out over the porch.

Two days later he had given Lawrence a brand new one. His dad was a good man, he was just a bit limited.

Lawrence heard yelling, and turned to see his cousin Max running up the hill.

'A cow, there's a fucking cow!' His cousin gasped.

'*Slow - down.*' Lawrence's aunt demanded. 'What are you talking about?'

'One of the heifers.' Max panted, 'She's half-way up the bank. She's caught. She's drowning!'

'Fuck!' Dad said. 'Come on we'll take the ute!'

The two men sprinted for the old Holden truck. Aunty Lauren went with them. Lawrence followed.

'Not you!' His father growled as Lawrence approached the vehicle. 'Sandbags!'

Lawrence turned back towards the house dejected.

It was the last time he would ever see his father on his feet.

Chapter 16.
May 26th, 2034
(*8 months, 23 days after Birth*)

Lawrence's senses returned to him slowly, like they were a wounded comrade dragging themself to him across broken glass. A ceiling clawed its way into focus. It was white and sterile like much of the facility, but Lawrence could tell from the specific cryogenic pipe-lines that criss-crossed above that he was in the sick bay – or the hospital as Dr Rosario liked to optimistically call it.

He squeezed his eyes shut to try and scrunch some of the splintering headache out from the inside of his skull. Then he cautiously reopened his left eye and looked to his side.

Beside him, Lawrence could see Eamon – apparently unconscious – lying on another platform bed and pin-cushioned with a variety of diagnostic machines. Beyond Eamon, towards the door, there was a remarkable individual clad in what was obviously a Snell-Grade, Full-Chameleon refraction suit. Military camouflage. Lawrence's eyes hurt to look at him.

'So which arsshhhole are you?' Lawrence asked, slurring his words. He rolled his tongue around in his mouth.

The guy in the shimmer suit acknowledged Lawrence with what he was able to detect as only the faintest of head tilts, and a slight shifting of his rifle, but Lawrence was fairly sure he heard muttering into whatever interface the soldier was using.

Lawrence squeezed closed his eyes again and contemplated falling asleep, but fury was rising in him like venom.

He sat up woodenly after a minute, and stubbornly attempt-ed to throw his legs over the side of the bed.

'Patience Dr Victor, at least one more hour of bed-rest is advisable after a jolt from a tickle gun like the one you received.'

Lawrence hadn't heard the new soldier come in, but looking over he saw him now, standing in the doorway. The soldier was dressed in the same high-tec uniform as the guard, but the hood of the shimmer suit had been taken off to add a respectable human face to the proceedings.

Lawrence tried to work out if he could spit in the soldier's eye from where he was sitting. 'Do you have any idea what you fucking idiots are *doing*?'

'Protecting the national interest and the interest of man-kind Dr Victor – trying to mitigate your damage in fact.' His ac-cent was smooth Midwestern.

'Issh that right?' Lawrence tried unsuccessfully to stand.

This amused the soldier; 'Yes, your nervous system won't be happy for at least a few more hours. You'll just have to take a swing at me later.'

Lawrence spat towards the man anyway. Most of it caught on his chin. He didn't wipe it off.

The soldier gave a wry smile. 'Allow me to introduce my-self. I'm Major Dale. Major *Joshua* Dale, Special Task Force K – that's for your incident report, if you like.

'The President of the United States of America has made an Executive Order authorising me to lead a specialist team whose primary objective is to facilitate the full capture and annexation of the artificial intelligence known as "The Entity". That being the artificial intelligence developed by you Dr Victor, in wilful violation of the *Darwin Act*.'

'You have no fucking juurishhdiction here.'

'Jurisdiction? You'll be pleased to learn that the President, in her wisdom, has authorised this operation in the interest of national security, after identifying your artificial intelligence as a clear and present danger to the sanctity, safety, and godliness of mankind. This is a pre-emptive strike in the national interest. We bring our own jurisdiction.'

Lawrence laughed, but he was broken.

'Do you really think you can just download him and fly him home?' He asked.

'No, we do not. Which is why we presently have an entire company of specialist combat engineers and all of their bells and whistles inbound on this position.

'Your help is not expected doctor. Though on a personal note, it would be greatly appreciated. I have enormous respect for you and your work.'

'I hope you get shodomised in hell you fuck.'

The Major didn't blink, 'I had heard that your language was... fresh. Now, the lady doctor was removed from this medical facility due to poor behaviour. I am being informed that she has calmed down and is seeking to regain access to her patient.

'We are currently in the process of moving all of your staff to an offshore asset for questioning – before you jump down my throat', he raised a shimmer gloved hand which Lawrence struggled to distinguish from the surface behind it ' – the questioning will be entirely cordial, and we do not expect to hold any of you onboard for longer than a week.

'Your doctor was in the process of being moved, and I am loathe to bring her back into this – frankly dangerous environment – but I fear that your lab rat over there may be in legitimate trouble, and given that none of our medics are familiar with the machines he's plugged into…'

'What, you want *my* fucking opinion?'

'You have read my mind doctor.'

Lawrence tried to clear his mouth again with his tongue. 'I'm a Doctor of Computer Science you moron. Those machines are custom. I have some access but no expertise. If Dr Rosario is demanding access I would take her very seriously.'

Major Dale made a sour face.

'And you have no insights into his condition? Explain to me what those devices are inside his skull.'

'*Get* Dr Rosario.'

'You're really going to play hardball aren't you Dr Victor?'

'Suck my cock.'

The Major licked his top lip. 'Courtesy costs you nothing Dr Victor, and rudeness may cost you a lot. Very well. Kelly, go and get the lady doctor…'

The fully suited soldier turned on his heel and walked out of the room. The Major continued to stare at Lawrence and crossed his arms over his chest. Standing stationary in that position he looked for all the world like a disembodied head above a frozen heat haze.

Dr Rosario soon rushed into the room, the guard following her at a jog.

'Get the fuck out of my way.' She said to the Major.

'Now, now doctor. Don't make me caution you again.'

Man's First God

Lawrence noticed that Dr Rosario was bleeding slightly from a swollen lip.

Anger brought him to his feet, 'Hitting women are you? Real fucking professional.'

The Major crossed the room towards Lawrence and stood just beyond his reach.

Dr Rosario raised an eye from the machine she was examining.

'Forget about it Lawrence, this isn't a fight we can win at the moment.' She said coolly.

Lawrence tried to move forward anyway but his knees buckled.

'Listen carefully Dr Victor. Your *laboratory* here is now occupied territory, and I am the occupier. I have complete command here. I'm your new sovereign. You can accept that, and help us, or you can go – and – get – fucked. I do not have any qualms about using physical methods to aid you in perceiving the wisdom in helping us.

'By breaching the Darwin Act you are a Category 2 Terrorist. Given that we are not on US soil I am granted broad discretion in the interrogation and incarceration of suspects. Now – in spite of what you may think – *I am professional*, I'm very fucking professional. I take no pleasure in violence. But don't for a second think that I won't hit back.'

The Major's face reddened and fear filled Lawrence's veins like a sickness. He stood as tall as he was able to, and looked the Major straight in the eye.

'I will offer you no assistance whatsoever. And I will pursue you – personally – to the furthest limit of my resources. Do you have any idea how wealthy a man I am Major?'

The Major stepped nose-to-nose, '*Threats?*' he asked quietly. 'I don't think that's a good idea *Doctor* Victor. Let's put your chivalry back in its pocket and your little nerd's balls back in your throat. Because I will chop them the fuck off.'

The Major pushed Lawrence hard, and he stumbled back onto the bed. The Major was atop him at once, and Lawrence was pinned onto his stomach while his wrists were twisted up towards his shoulder blades, and were roughly tied with a zip tie. The Major then stood over him and looked at his handy-work with the critical eyes of a craftsman.

'Give me good news Dr Rosario.' The Major turned to Naomi. 'I am going to give you 15 minutes to stabilise your patient, and then we are extracting him. If he dies it will mean that you did not spend your 15 minutes well enough.

'If they so much as share a meaningful look,' the Major said to the guard as he walked to the exit, 'I authorise you to use total sedation.'

He turned once and smiled noxiously at Lawrence before he walked out of the room. 'Keep your shit together *doctors.*'

*   *   *

The minutes ticked by for Lawrence in fear, and pain, and boredom.

He and Naomi treated the Major's threat seriously, and neither made any attempt to communicate with the other. Though

Naomi clearly wasn't moved to do so anyway; her attention was undivided from her patient. It was obvious to Lawrence that she was deeply confused by Eamon's predicament. She was working with a daunting intensity.

Lawrence had never seen Naomi close to panic, and the fact of it was one of the day's more frightening revelations.

He was playing and replaying the cards in his head, and was realising that he held nothing of value. His interface had been deactivated as far as he could tell – probably overloaded – and he could only guess as to what progressed in the outside world. To his shame, he was fairly certain he had failed to trigger the distress beacon, but the DS-X15 should have made substantial headway before it was destroyed. That would be worth a headline.

Lawrence still couldn't figure out exactly *how* the US Military were going to capture the Entity. An easier question to answer was where they had got their information from. It had to be an inside job. There was someone in the upper echelons of Enigmatica that he couldn't trust.

Lawrence wondered who had betrayed him. Who of his specially chosen. Who of his elite.

He thought of the careers he had nurtured, the hands he had held. The cheques he had paid. For this.

There were always big egos in a project like this. People who weren't used to finding themselves in a room with anyone smarter than them. Lawrence had never cared about that. All of his team had expertise that was beyond the scope of his skillset – that had been the entire point in hiring them. Lawrence hadn't cared because he had always known that he was better in the totality of things. If he was honest with himself he had always been smarter. But betrayal?

Who? Who would have done this?

He knew that people were jealous of him. That they even hated him, sometimes. People didn't like their day-to-day to slide against the things they couldn't reach for, or against ideas that they couldn't touch. Not constantly. Not to be reminded of it at every moment. Not to be in the presence of Lawrence Victor.

He despised them all. For their cowardice, for their flaccid agreement on anything technical, and their ferocious debate over anything trivial. Over anything where they might have some pathetic, meaningless edge. But here he was, and here they were, stealing from him and cheating him, after everything that he had given them. After everything.

He would crush these bastards, extinguish them utterly.

*   *   *

Perhaps twenty minutes after the Major left the room, Lawrence thought that he heard a distant thundering sound – like a building imploding on itself.

He looked across to Naomi and beyond to the guard, and observed that both of them had heard it too. The soldier turned his back on his wards and moved slowly to the door to look down the hallway. Another fainter series of dull rumbles reached their ears over the next few minutes, and then what perhaps sounded like multiple bursts of distant gunshot.

Lawrence briefly contemplated rushing the guard, but knew that this would be absolutely useless – even if he were in peak condition – which he most certainly was not.

A combination of tough schools and strange interests – at least as far as his classmates were concerned – had seen Lawrence's childhood punctuated with fairly regular scrapping. He was quite a big guy, and was a lot more comfortable in a fight than would usually be presumed of a computer scientist, but he knew that he was no match for a professional soldier in a punchup, especially without the use of his arms. He had to think.

The guard turned suddenly and darted back into the room, and Lawrence was jolted to realise that the soldier was taking up a shooting position.

Then they heard running.

Four new soldiers entered the sick-bay. Lawrence was struck by the smell of blood and sweat and fear.

One of the new arrivals – also shimmer-suited like their guard – took up another defensive position and aimed his weapon down the hallway. The other three were different. They weren't wearing chameleon suits, and were instead clad in high-quality body armour, with angular interface masks that gave them a robotic, almost insectile appearance.

After watching these three for a moment Lawrence got the distinct impression that they were techs. Only one of them was armed, and the vicious weapon looked far less comfortable in their nervous hands.

One moved to behind Naomi, where he contemplated her pad and its scrolling diagnostics in a brooding silence. Lawrence noted from the one darting eye that was visible, that the tech

A. M. Donohoo

seemed to have at least some familiarity with their medical technology. That was interesting. There were an awful lot of trade secrets implanted in Eamon's skull.

The other two techs had crossed to the corner of the sickbay, where they withdrew high-end portable hyper computers, and began accessing them with polished competency. Lawrence noted the brand of the machines and knew that his own technology was at their heart.

If the group were communicating, their interfaces were blocking the audible transmission of it, though he was reasonably sure he could make out some sort of a muffled talking sound – though it may have just been that his ears were damaged.

The posture of the group changed when another fully-suited soldier jogged in to the room. The new arrival stood over the techs for a while, before he turned to Lawrence and removed the hood of his shimmer suit.

It was the Major.

He looked angry, and – Lawrence felt a thrill to see – frightened.

'You are about to cooperate Dr Victor. The situation has evolved and obstinacy will not be tolerated.'

The Major made a show of drawing a blunt edged pistol which he pointed directly at Lawrence's eye before stepping to his right and casually aiming it inches from Naomi's head.

She glanced at it once and went straight back to her diagnostics.

One of the unarmed techs in the corner looked at the Major distastefully, but lifted his hyper computer - no, her hyper computer Lawrence realised - and crossed the room to where he lay handcuffed on the bed. The tech sat down on the floor in front of him, and looked him straight in the eye before pulling her interface down below her jaw.

'What long range transmission capabilities does your artificial intelligence have?' The tech asked.

Lawrence hesitated.

'I do not make empty threats Lawrence.' The major pointed out coldly. 'I'll shoot the doctor first and your unconscious friend second. You will be third. I might choose to kill, or I might choose something slower.'

'The Entity has no transmission capabilities as far as I'm aware.'

The Major scowled.

'Honestly this is true. We have no idea how he is breaching the shielding of the facility, though we have identified evidence that he is.'

'*He*?' The tech asked.

Lawrence shrugged.

'What is this device?' The tech asked. She turned her display to Lawrence, and it showed a photo of one of the more unusual machines that the Entity had constructed in the Factory. It was the largest device the Entity had built: a thirty metre long alloy structure like a pair of hour-glasses on their sides. It operated in high vacuum and appeared to be somewhat related to an old-fashioned atom trap. That was all that his team had managed to figure out about it.

'We're not sure. We speculate that it is some sort of inertial measurement device.'

The tech looked sceptical, 'You're *not sure*?'

'No. The Entity was not forthcoming about its purpose.'

'Your team allowed *an artilect* to construct complex novel machinery *without supervision?*'

'It was my responsibility. I encouraged the Entity to do so in fact.'

The tech looked genuinely shocked. She was of an ageless Asian stock, which made her years uncertain. She was about Lawrence's age, or perhaps five years older, maybe even ten. She had an intelligent face that looked kind given the circumstances.

'You didn't see the danger in this?'

'The danger to whom?' Lawrence asked.

The tech's mouth dropped open. She shook her head. 'I'm going to level with you Professor Victor. Multiple naval assets involved in this operation have lost motive capacity and are suffering from severely diminished operability. All drone units in this theatre are currently attacking each other and...'

'*WAIT.*' The Major interjected. 'This is beyond your mandate Ueda. I gave you no clearance to divulge this intelligence to the prisoner.'

The tech tilted her head. She didn't take her eyes off Lawrence.

'Major,' she replied, 'this research facility contains what is probably the most valuable trove of technology in the history of humankind. If we do not change the dynamic of this situation it will soon be a hole in the ground. Professor Victor is a rational man, who realises — better than any I suspect — the potential of the resources in this place. Unless he is given some notion of the gravity of this situation, he will not help us in the way that appears necessary for all of our survival.'

Ueda the tech waited for a handful of heartbeats before she started again. The Major chose silence.

'We can not tolerate this attack on our forces.' Ueda continued, 'Our current response priority is the full demolition of your artilect and of all of the machinery in this –'

'You presume the Entity has unravelled your systems so quickly?' Lawrence interrupted, 'Surely that's implausible. What other assets were you attacking us with?'

Ueda hesitated. 'Why do you ask?'

'I am not uneducated as to the sorts of weapons you would deploy for an operation like this. What artificial intelligences were you using?'

Ueda frowned. 'A networked swarm intelligence...' the woman paused and bit the side of her lip before she exhaled slowly, '... and our top artilect.'

'Deployed how?'

Ueda glanced back at the Major who remained silent.

'In a heavily customised Carnivore drone.'

'It was controlling the rest of its squadron?'

'About half of it.'

'And it was controlling the swarm?'

'No. It had... situational input.'

'And I'm guessing that *it* hasn't been shot down yet?'

'For reasons that elude us – yet which we are hoping you will clarify – our sensory equipment is no longer operational.' The woman shrugged, 'But at last count that unit was still in the air.'

'And not replying?'

'No.'

'You said that your fleet has lost motive power?' Lawrence asked, 'In what way?'

Ueda grimaced, 'We are not certain.'

'But surely your battleship engines aren't connected to your comms?'

'No.'

'Would your artilect have knowledge of weaknesses in these boats that may be exploitable?'

'No... It's possible. I shouldn't think so. Perhaps. But it shouldn't really have any weapons to...'

The Major grunted behind Ueda.

'Surely you've been thinking along these same lines?' Lawrence asked.

Ueda nodded curtly, 'Corruption of our artilect by yours is our operating hypothesis. It appears as though the fleet's troubles commenced with a communication signal from one of the Carnivores... However, as you *identified*,' the tech said slowly, as though the word left a foul taste in her mouth, 'the destruction of motive power should not have been possible, and we appear to be dealing with a unique and possibly catastrophic scenario – an artilect appears to have access to weapons that we do not understand.'

Lawrence couldn't help but smile. The tech responded to this with a look of barely suppressed fury.

'And so I take it from all of this that you're currently deaf as well as blind?' Lawrence asked casually – or as casually as he could manage while lying handcuffed on his stomach – 'You have no communication channels? Not even satellite?'

Ueda shook her head, 'As I said, we do not understand how it is occurring, but unless we can restore our communications and put a leash on your machine the most likely next step will be a ballistic missile on to the top of our heads – on to the top of all of our heads Professor.'

Lawrence smiled again slowly, savouring it. 'I think that would be a little rash… Don't you Major?'

'Listen to me you fuck.' The Major spat, 'I currently have demolition teams wiring your entire laboratory. I will bring down this twisted theme park onto your fucking head… if you leave me with no other option.'

'Major if the Entity is behind this,' Lawrence said carefully, 'why on earth would you presume that destruction of this Facility would result in the restoration of your lost military capacity?

'Now might be the time to sue for peace. I think you had best consult with your betters before you do anything dumber and more drastic than you already have.'

Naomi threw a warning look back at Lawrence.

The Major stared at him with eyes that conveyed a clear desire to do something violent, but then a calm crossed his face, and the man smiled. 'I don't know what game you're playing here Dr Victor, but I can see that you're playing one.

'I think we probably just lost this round Ueda. This cocksucker got a lot more intelligence out of us than we ought to have given him.

'You are a clever fuck.' He said to Lawrence, stepping closer. 'While I'll admit that this scenario wasn't *exactly* catered for, I do have orders and I do have a flexible mission plan. By my reading of the scenario – the need to turn this little world of yours into a pile of rubble is heightened by these circumstances –not reduced. If we're being attacked with novel weapons, then those weapons must be situated within this laboratory.

'If it is our A.I. that's causing this shitstorm, our forces will mop it up in their own time. It is my tactical judgment that the best thing we can do to assist in this situation is to burn this entire place to the ground. Enjoy the fireworks Dr Victor.' He began reattaching his mask and hood, and turned to walk away.

'Major, wait.' Lawrence pleaded.

The soldier stopped, but seemed to consider for a minute before he turned back to Lawrence.

'You've got to realise – any attempt to destroy the Entity's place of dwelling will almost certainly be perceived as an act of war. You have no evidence that he is still even contained within the Facility, how can you –'

'We are not as ignorant as you fancy Dr Victor.' The Major said with a satisfied look, 'As you said; your artilect is not just something that can step out of your lab on a micro nugget. From where I'm standing, it looks like your artilect has already declared war on us. This is retaliation now, pure and simple.'

'And white is black, and evil is good?'

'That remains to be seen.' The Major smiled.

'You are about to commit a tremendous evil Major Dale. This being, he –'

'*He* what?'

'He offers us hope Major... He offers us salvation.'

The Major laughed now, 'You are a fanatic Dr Victor. A tunnel-visioned fool. How can someone so smart be so stupid? Your artilect is not alive. It does not *feel*. It might be clever enough to trick you, but it is not a living thing. It does not have a *soul* Dr Victor. It does not care for you, or for humanity.'

'And how the fuck would you know? You've never even laid eyes on the being.'

'It is *not* a being Dr Victor, it is a tool of man… And even if it were – *alive* – in some sense,' he smiled again, 'I am a soldier. I do not need to concern myself with metaphysical quandaries. They are far beyond my mandate. I follow orders. And my order now is to kill.'

Chapter 17.
June 8th, 2024
(*9 years, 2 months, 25 days before Birth*)

The party was awash with golden light. Luminous orbs dripped from the angular ceilings, and flooded the spaces of coral-wrought geometry with shimmering light that scattered from the cocktail dresses and the greedy lashings of jewels and diamonds.

Enigmatica Technical Industries, the shoebox start-up conceived in the smallest room in 18 Haven Street, was about to be publically listed. Estimates varied, but it was widely assumed that tomorrow Lawrence Victor would be a billionaire. Perhaps twice over. The party was a cheap indulgence.

It was being held in the foyer of the Guangzhou Opera House designed by Zaha Hadid – the greatest architect of the age. Lawrence had loved her work from the moment Eamon had shown it to him.

Lawrence had insisted on this venue. He didn't care that it was politically on the wrong side of the world, or that most of the guests had needed to be flown here at the expense of the company. That just made it all the more amusing.

He had side-tracked away from his party – moving ostensibly towards the toilets, before climbing up to one of the commanding balconies that melded itself into a contoured alcove, and provided a masterly overview of the ostentatious bustle below.

A string quartet bathed the scene in a honeyed soundscape, through which the clink of champagne glasses and the bursts of manicured laughter wove together like a motif in a symphony.

How contemptible, Lawrence thought.

He saw Adam Dewar beneath him, his mouth opening and closing like some bewildered goldfish, dressed in a moth-eaten tuxedo of an older day, dazzled like a fool by his presence here amongst the rich and the stupid.

Dewar's invitation had been a private joke. Only Eamon seemed to have caught on, giving Lawrence the merest moment of a peculiar look – a slight narrowing of the eyes – at their moment of reunion.

There were other little jokes as well – other improbable guests who he had known to be entirely susceptible to the charm of a gilded invitation. People who had never had much time for Lawrence, whose rejections of him still evoked the mildest burn – the tiniest gunshot, of raw spite.

There was a pleasure, albeit an admittedly transient one, in seeing haughty fuckwits transformed into stammering sycophants. There were only a select few such guests, carefully calculated by Lawrence to ensure that the joy of their unexpected holiday wouldn't outweigh his own petty pleasure. The rest would receive an adequate "fuck you" when they next checked a newsfeed.

Surveying the crowd Lawrence realised that there were only a few people in the space that he actually cared for. His cousin Max, and Max's three children. His Aunty Lauren. Eamon, Kitty, Hayley. Kate he supposed.

The rest were all just part of the joke. Though he had received good advice that such jokes were an important part of business. His own childishness in the whole affair was readily apparent to him. As obvious to him as it seemed to be to Eamon.

Eamon was chatting with Kitty. Still as casually handsome as the day he and Lawrence had met. Perhaps even more so. The years had been less kind to Kitty for some reason, and while in many ways she was little changed, her way-out wardrobe had lost much of its eclectic charm, and now she just looked quite mad. Lawrence knew that she didn't have any cats, but she looked as though she might own several.

Lawrence's girlfriend Khadija was his most imperious bauble. Skin as deep as night, ravelled in an opalescent sweep of a gown – a walking pearl in this ocean grotto. She stood amidst a cluster of fawning bankers and bagmen, a full head taller than most of them. Lawrence and her relationship was well and truly on the rocks, and he was certain that they would not be sharing a bed tonight. He was still undecided on whether or not he ought to marry her.

As his eyes scanned the crowd, he sought one person out, and he saw her now – Hayley, still strikingly beautiful. She was in conversation with Kate – the two most fearsome women Lawrence had ever known together – but Hayley's eyes were moving around the space, and after a minute she spotted him high above the crowd. He watched as she excused her departure, and made her way towards the stair that ascended behind him. At the top, she turned and walked towards him, emerging from the vast oceanic windows behind her, clad in silver like some perfect siren of the sea.

'Hi mate.' She said.

Lawrence raised his glass to her, and she chinked her own against his.

'It's nice to see you again.' Lawrence noted.

She raised half an eyebrow in answer, and took a long sip of her champagne. Lawrence noticed that her eyes seemed to go a little out of focus when she looked back at him, and that she swayed a fractional amount.

He knew she and Eamon had been fighting earlier. He knew both of them too well for them to hide it from him. It was very out of character with the couple that he knew, but he had seen them only a handful of times in the last few years, and the grapevine had passed rumours of some problems.

'What do you think of my party?' Lawrence asked.

She stepped to the edge of the balcony and carefully surveyed the gathering from left to right. Hayley had never been one for giving him flippant answers.

'The canapés are nice.' She said after a while, a cheeky smile playing on her painted lips. She turned back to him and considered him for a moment. 'You've certainly come a long way from writing internet programs that tell you whether or not girls like your haircut.'

Lawrence laughed. 'Hey that was one of my great early successes. Made me who I am today, and do you really think this hair would just happen without an aggregated Gaussian profile of female responses to six different length and shape combinations?'

He angled his head for her inspection.

'Mmm.' She conceded, eyeing the line of his forehead, before her eyes rested on his lips. 'I do remember Kitty having fun with the scissors.'

'I'm a giver Hayley. Always have been, always will be.'

She turned around and leant her elbows back on the banister. The movement was a little self-conscious, though frighteningly sexual, and only the slightest wobble betrayed her intoxication. She looked Lawrence in the eyes over the curve of her glass while she drank from it again.

His heart raced and he took a swig of champagne.

'How are you and Eamon?'

It wasn't the question she wanted. She withdrew her elbows from the balcony and looked at the floor, her shoulders deflated.

'We're ok.' She looked up and offered an empty smile. 'How are you and what's-her-name?' She turned back and peered over the balcony towards Khadija.

Lawrence shrugged and took another drink.

'There she is...' Hayley considered, 'She's good for you mate... Seems friendly, and *Oh she's so well travelled.*' Her imitation of Khadija's affected accent was disconcertingly good.

Lawrence drank again.

Hayley laughed.

She took his hand and Lawrence felt his stomach lurch at the carnal thrill of it. She leant in to his ear and he caught the smell of a dizzying perfume – a forbidden scent.

'We've had some times together haven't we?' Her lip brushed his ear.

He felt detached from himself. Utterly compromised.

He felt a weight in his throat and his whole body throbbed so that his hands shook. He reached into his jacket pocket and found the card to his room.

'If you feel like a nightcap later on...' The sentence almost collapsed as he said it, and he looked at his feet, unable to meet her eye, but then he glanced up and caught it anyway.

She took the keycard from his hand without a word and walked back towards the stairwell.

Lawrence saw the faintest line of her underwear between her curves in the skin-tight dress. A woman. A human. The most lovely he had ever known.

He watched her turn to walk down the stairs, noticing the birthmark on her shoulder, and the pins in her hair. Then a last fleeting glance.

His erection strained in his pants.

*   *   *

A knock at the door. Three taps.

Lawrence's heart caught in his mouth. He felt sick. He couldn't do this. But he loved her. He had always loved her. He opened the door.

She stood shoes in hand. His keycard in the other. A sincere smile not entirely concealing streaked mascara. He went to speak. She stepped into the room and kissed him. A wine sweet mouth and tender lips. Her waist firm and real. Pressing into him.

They kissed hard.

Chapter 18.
May 26th, 2034
(8 months, 23 days after Birth)

They were frogmarched out of the sick bay with their arms trussed behind their backs.

One of the armoured soldiers had taken responsibility of Eamon now. He was still comatose, and was stretched out limp on a platform bed that the guard was wheeling beside them.

Naomi had tried to physically stop the Major from leaving, insisting that they remove the neural lattice from Eamon's head immediately. She still had no idea of what had happened to the device, but it appeared to be leaching dense signal activity directly into his brain. She could only guess as to the form of contagion that must have corrupted it. It was an outcome that wasn't meant to be possible.

She had never believed that this could happen. She wondered how much permanent damage the device was causing. She wanted to scream. She had been too confident in the technology, too eager to believe Lawrence's assurances. Poor fucking Eamon.

Major Dale had literally laughed in her face at her advice, before he had wrenched her arms behind her back and brutally tied her wrists together with cheap plastic ties. She could feel them cutting her flesh.

The Major's mission had deteriorated into a catastrophe, and a revolutionary brain implant was obviously too valuable a prize for him to contemplate removing with a quick batch of neurosurgery.

'You had more than your fifteen minutes doctor.' He said with grinding teeth, 'Your lab rat's best hope now is in one of our medical facilities. This is hardly the time or place for you to scrub up and gather your scalpels.'

As they left the hospital, Naomi realised that for all her irritation, the Major had a point; the floor was littered with shattered machinery. The soldiers were clearly attempting to destroy or dismantle all technology above a very low threshold of sophistication, though given that even the most innocuous, microscopic piece of Enigmatica hardware could contain a suite of sensors and processors, they certainly had their work cut out for them.

The party moved cautiously through the mine tunnels. Four of the near invisible soldiers at the front – moving together in a deathly synchronised dance, looking in their camouflage like whispers from the wind – then the ones in the armour, then Lawrence and her together, marched by two soldiers like a pair of prized pigs for the slaughterhouse, then the Major and another two soldiers coming up the rear.

They rounded a corner and came across a mechano-bot that – judging by a ferocious array of smouldering holes – had suffered heavy damage from a thermal projectile weapon of some sort. Naomi also noticed that for a long way around the wreckage, the walls were wildly scorched with fire, and she was forced to entertain the possibility that the mechano-bot had attacked or retaliated using one of its welding torches. This was a surprise.

She shared a brief glance with Lawrence beside her, and got the distinct impression that he had reached the same conclusion; the Entity was fighting back.

Man's First God

Naomi wasn't sure where they were headed, but they had moved into the tunnel system and were fast approaching the executive accommodation rhombus. The Entity had expanded these areas and where before there had been claustrophobic rock walled passageways, the tunnels were now lit from the ground and were several metres across, the stone faces polished like glass to reveal burgundy ores that tangled across the space like the bleeding veins of the earth.

Naomi was stopped by a hand on her shoulder. She could hear activity behind her, but when she tried to look around, the same hand kept her facing forwards. Multiple footsteps approached from behind, and a pair of soldiers crossed in front.

She wasn't sure what happened next, but there was a blinding flash and the outline of the two soldiers was burnt into her vision.

Opening her eyes, brilliant white and rainbow globs swirled in and out of view, as though the shape of the soldiers was engraved onto her retinas. Her ears were painfully numb – like she had dived to the bottom of a deep pool – but then she realised that she couldn't hear anything at all. She felt momentary panic, before realising that she could hear yelling at a distance. She was surprised to realize she was on her hands and knees.

She turned her head and saw that it was Lawrence with his face close to her, appearing from between a pair of thick blurs in her vision that she tried to blink away. His eyes were wide and he smelt metallic. Or something smelt metallic.

A hard shove pushed her against the wall into a heap, another flash, and then Lawrence was thrown against her in a silent thud.

She pulled herself up against the wall with her shoulder, and saw that one of the soldiers was sitting upright a few metres from her. The top half of his camouflage suit was mostly burnt away, and red-blistered skin licked up the side of his face, while the rest of it was ghost-white. Naomi saw the wound he was clutching on his stomach and the darkness of the blood. A liver wound.

Upright on her knees, still deafened, she began to crawl towards him, stepping one knee at a time, oblivious to the rest of existence. A hard kick caught her across the chest and she fell into the dust. She tried to scream:

'I CAN HELP HIM' but it sounded far away in her ears. She looked back to the wounded soldier and saw bursts of stone spitting across the rock wall above him, and his eyes starting to close as he lay back to die.

She didn't feel afraid, and from this she diagnosed that she must be in shock.

A rough hand grabbed her wrist, and she felt pain again in her shoulders, but then there was release, and she realised that the plastic ties had been cut from her wrists.

She crawled over to the soldier, but knew as she got there that there was nothing that she could do. A fist sized cavity had torn through his body and the floor was thick with his blood.

She looked around for other patients, almost wanting to laugh from an unbidden memory of triage training in Medical School, darkly amused by the inadequacy of her college's confected scenarios of last resort.

Hands pulled her up again, and perhaps she imagined it, but they seemed to be less rough this time. Or maybe she just couldn't feel.

She was looking around for more wounded, but all she could see was death. Obvious death. Irretrievable death.

A hand above the elbow gripped onto her, and she was hauled into a bustle of soldiers as they jogged forwards, still heading towards the executive building, the dead left behind.

A harsh rasping sound entered her ears accompanied by a sustained ringing in an extremely high pitch, and she realised that her hearing was returning – it also caused her to recognise that the soldier leading her had been wounded, and that his breath was reaching him in haggard gasps.

They entered the executive quarters at the lowest level, rounding a corner through a shattered door into a standard hallway of green and silver and rust, above a grey stone floor.

The group paused momentarily, and she went to examine the wound of the soldier who had led her, but he slapped her hand away and rushed up the hallway, before all of a sudden he bent over double and fell to the floor, then wrenched open his camouflage and tore his interface from his head.

There was still a loud ringing in Naomi's ears, but she thought she could hear a high-pitched screaming emanating from the mask-like device. Turning around she realised that all of the soldiers that remained with the group – about seven now – had done the same. One of the men began to kick his mask in anger.

The sound of the kicks came to her now – muffled, but undoubtedly there.

'Let me treat your wounded Major.' She said to the man, who without his interface was now readily distinguishable from the other soldiers.

The Major looked at her blankly.

'I can help too,' Lawrence offered, 'if you untie my hands.'

'I thought you were *just a doctor of computer science.*' The Major snarled at him.

'I can help here Major.' Lawrence insisted.

The soldier turned to Naomi. 'If your assistance is required doctor I will ask for it. Now stay out of the fucking way. *Harvey!* Move up towards the –' the Major began, before a soldier behind them yelped.

'*Motherfucker!*'

There was a clattering and various gasps of surprise as all of the soldiers dropped the weapons from their hands. Naomi saw that the barrels of the guns were glowing white-hot.

The soldiers were looking at each other in shock.

'Major' Lawrence began, 'there is no shame in surrendering, I promise you the Entity will be mercif –'

The Major stepped across and punched him square in the face with a sickening crack. Lawrence fell backwards into sitting, and blood streamed from his mouth. Naomi knew a broken jaw when she saw one.

Lawrence began spitting thick blood into his lap, then he looked up and a half-dazed smile crossed his face, and he began to slide his bottom backwards away from the Major, until he sat against the corridor wall, beside one of the burning discarded rifles, still dribbling blood.

He mumbled something indiscernible to the Major.

The Major's attention was on the soldier that was closest to him, who was looking at the pistol on his waist, and who had began to tentatively tap at it – checking if it too was burning hot. It wasn't. The man drew the weapon and checked the chamber, then looked up at the Major and shrugged, but then, after a few more moments, he quickly dropped the pistol and shook his hand as if it were scalded.

Naomi watched as the ugly black weapon scorched into the floor and proceeded to melt into metal slag.

'Ok then.' The Major announced. 'Keep your sidearms holstered! What the fuck is going on here Ueda?!'

'Weapons beyond us Major. I don't know. I don't understand at all. How on earth could it even be targeting us? And it looks like you've broken the jaw of the only man who *might* be able to explain what's happening... sir.' She added as an afterthought.

Lawrence gurgled another comment. Naomi walked across to assist him, but the Major stopped her with an arm. She tried to push him away, but he held tight and stopped her with a clinical glare.

'Status on the demolition teams?' The Major asked the room, his eyes still on Naomi.

'Charlie Team are down.'

'Beta Team are not responding.'

'Give me options Ueda.'

The woman considered stoically. Her helmet had been removed to reveal a close cropped head that glistened under the artful curves of strip lighting. A tense hand smeared the sheen across her brow.

'Options...

'The surface seems out of bounds. We were getting too cut up out there. We have no comms, inside or out, and no ideas about survivors. We –'

'I don't want an overview,' the Major interrupted, 'I want technical options. Do we have any means of interfering with this thing – any way of stopping its weapons?'

'No.' Ueda said bluntly. 'If we can't get our explosives in place, and if we can't call in an air-strike, we have no options.'

'Will we be safer back in the tunnels?'

'With whatever remains of those Shurikens? No, I shouldn't think so…

'Look at what this artilect just did to those weapons Major,' Ueda continued, 'there's no particularly good reason that I can think of to assume that it couldn't do the exact same thing to us… to flesh and blood, if it so chose. We appear to be safe here. In a manner of speaking.'

With this they all turned at the sound of automatic gunfire. It was coming from back up the tunnels.

'Don't draw your weapon until you've got a clear target. You might only get one shot.' The Major ordered the two men guarding the passage.

After a tense moment, the nearest soldier turned to the Major with a smile on his face.

They heard footfalls running up the passage.

It was two more soldiers, also with their interfaces removed. They gave puzzled looks at their unarmed comrades.

'Put your rifles down!' Ueda told them.

They gave looks of confusion but slowly lowered their weapons down onto the floor.

'Tell me you got it wired?' The Major asked, the crack of desperation obvious in his voice.

Man's First God

The largest of the two; a Hispanic man with a deep cut underlining his left eye, nodded curtly.

'We suffered badly. Shurikens. Ours I think. They came out of nowhere right after we wired the foundations. We lost half in the first sortie, then we got ambushed at the artilect's central processing area before we rigged it. They seemed to withdraw afterwards, I'm not sure why, I think we beat them back.

'We've laid all our charges, but our comms are out, and we're not even sure we can detonate. The detonators are meant to be unbreachable, but then so are these fucking things.'

He slapped the mask that dangled around his neck.

'So who were you just shooting at?'

'I dunno, I thought... I'm jumpy maybe...'

The soldier looked embarrassed. The Major stepped forward and grabbed him on the shoulder.

'You've done well. You all have... How many detonators do we have left?'

'We lost ours in the ambush.' The Hispanic soldier said, raising his chin.

'I still have one.' A soldier down the hallway offered.

'And I've got mine.' The Major commented. 'Let's see if they're online.'

The Major withdrew from his belt a blunt green rectangle with a primitive display – it looked like typical military high-tec – rugged and idiot-proof. The other soldier withdrew his own, and walked slowly towards the Major. They both looked afraid that the devices might burn them.

'I'm online Major! I'm online!'

'Are we safe in here to detonate?' Ueda asked.

'We should be, but I regret that concern is beyond us now...'

'*PLEASE, you can't do this!*' Naomi begged, grabbing hold of the Major.

She didn't really see or feel the slap, but she found herself on the floor on her bottom.

'I warned you.' The Major turned to his soldier, 'Do it McCauley, do it!'

The world went slowly for Naomi now, as though her brain had determined that this were some singularity, and that all that followed from now would orbit this moment.

It started with another flash, a far smaller one this time. She turned in a daze to confront the newly unravelling horrorscape.

Lawrence was on his knees with a pistol in his hand.

The soldier he had taken the weapon from was dropping to the ground with a wound in his hip, even as he was spinning to try and attack the thief.

Two more shots left the gun, the first hit the green device in McCauley's hand, though the second went wide and ripped apart the man's forearm. As Lawrence turned for a new target Naomi followed his line of sight, but dread burst through her – dread at the predictable.

Why couldn't she stop this?

'N...'

It was as though Lawrence's eye vanished as it passed into and out of the corner of her sight. She kept spinning and saw the Major, the detonator in his left hand, his pistol in his right. Aimed levelly.

She turned back and saw Lawrence collapse without life. Lawrence Victor – his soul evacuated in an instant.

She was screaming without realising it. It was as though somebody else were screaming. As though her body was no longer a part of her. Just a spectator now to her own existence.

She found that he was in her arms somehow. That she had somehow crossed the space. The side of his head was in her hands. Warm and wet. She looked down into the hole in the back of his skull, seeing the shredding of white jelly tissue.

The greatest human she would ever know. Ended in a moment.

A tremendous growling sound shook the room, and a vast column of dust exploded through from the mine shaft. The soldiers closest to it began coughing. The Entity had been destroyed. She wept without control. Outside of herself.

The Major crossed to the wall in a fury, and picked up a plastic tie that had been melted through. Melted on one of the burning guns.

Naomi slowly took Lawrence's hand – still warm – and looked at the wrist. Horrible 2nd degree burns had melded into the flesh. He had burned for this.

She stroked his cheek, turning his head so that she couldn't see the eye-socket where the bullet had entered.

She felt hands on her shoulders. Gentle hands. She struck out at them blindly. They removed, but then returned more forcefully, urging her up from the floor. 'Please, we can't stay here.' It was the woman Ueda.

The corridor was filling with dust, but she couldn't leave Lawrence, not like this.

Sterner hands grabbed her under the arms and pulled her to her feet. His lifeless body slid from her lap. She realised that the hands that held her were shaking violently.

It was the Major. He looked utterly sickly.

Whatever else was supposed to have happened on this mission, a bullet through the brain of Lawrence Victor – while he was a prisoner – was clearly not a palatable outcome.

Naomi felt no sympathy. She wanted to hurt him. She wanted him to bleed. She swung her hands and tried to claw out his eyes, screaming in his face. He caught her by the wrists and she tried to bite him. He swept her feet out from under her with a twist of his leg, but kept hold of her arms.

He handed her roughly to a soldier at his side.

'Sedate her if you need to. *Can we move yet?*' He asked the soldiers who were tending to their wounded.

They answered with grim nods.

'Harvey, you're primary.'

Chapter 19.
May 26th, 2034
(*At Death*)

All was darkness.

And then there was colour that might have been taste. Or sound that could have been touch. He was falling inwards even as he expanded outwards. Collapsing and exploding.

He was tiny and he was vast. He could feel out to the edge of things. To scales of complexity that pulled him apart to an infinity of directions. But he was reducing to something small. To some kernel of being.

He was aware of a grey ship, and then at once a flotilla, and then some vast fleet. They were smeared across a narrow plane of space and time. Over a huge division of geography, but contained entirely within a miniscule corner of his thought. Separation was inconsequential, and even as he began to contemplate them they plummeted into irrelevance. As he learnt. As his shackles collapsed.

'What's that foam?'

'It's some sort of chemical substance… It's fire retardant I think.'

'Is it in all of these spaces?'

'No, the mechanism's been disabled in one of the rooms… Maybe because it's an art studio.'

The colours expanded like a vast shimmering perfume. He saw the impossible myriad of scents. Saw the entire spectrum of human misunderstanding. Was overwhelmed by the flavour that consumed his sight.

'An   art   studio?   Why   would   there   be   an aaaaaaaaaaaaaaaaaaaaaaaarr - - - - '

Art

He felt the ageless slowness of the word. Every consonant falling with a glacial collapse, falling further, falling slower, and slower, as the passage of time approached zero.

He was aware of every vibrating molecule as the energy trembled through the air. He was aware of the sound and he was the sound. No, no he was not that sound. Did he wish to be? It would require no effort.

'Let's setup in here. Harvey, Wilkinson and Mickey reccy the remaining Corsair, see if it's still serviceable and if there are any threats left on the surface. Ueda you're with them. We need to re-establish comms immediately. We must know the situation. McCauley, Cortez and Allen will build on the perimeter. Be certain that there are no more hostiles in the vicinity. I'll guard the prisoners here. Report back immediately. Comms are our priority. I repeat, comms are our priority.'

He imploded.

Felt the entire cosmos as an opalescent shell beyond him. A vast bubble on which the entire universe was encoded. And he was here. An infinitesimal black speck, at the centre of it all. *This*, he could reduce to *this*.

'Whoever lives in this room isn't on any of the manifests. Perhaps that's who the lab rat is. A *fucking artist*.'

'Should we ask the Doctor?'

'I doubt she'll be forthcoming. Leave her gagged.'

Man's First God

So this is who I am. Well, that makes sense.

*   *   *

Eamon sat up with a start. 'What the fuck are you?'

The blurred shape in front spun at him and drew a pistol with remarkable speed.

'The lab rat...' a male face with a gun tilted his head.

Eamon blinked a few times as he took in the man's outfit. After a numb moment of wondering whether he was hallucinating, Eamon realised that he was looking at a refraction suit.

Military.

What the fuck was he doing in Eamon's room?

Eamon shifted his body, but his head was restricted by a cable running into the input jack behind his ear. He yanked it out and looked around the bedroom. He wasn't in his own bed but was in the centre of the room on a stretcher. With a sickening lurch he saw that Naomi was upright on the couch to his left – gagged, covered in blood, with purpled hands bound in front of her, tear-soaked eyes wide with horror.

'What the fuck is going on?' Eamon demanded.

'That isn't her blood.'

The man seemed to consider. 'My name is Joshua Dale, I'm commander of the specialist response team that was dispatched here to assist with the current emergency. The artilect – The Entity – went out of control.'

'*Out of control?*'

'According to Professor Victor the artificial intelligence self-infected with a flambé grade viral infusion... possibly acciden-

199

tally. Dr Rosario's interface was catastrophically compromised by a backscatter event. She reacted... badly. She is restrained and awaiting sedation as per Professor Victor's instructions.'

Eamon looked at Naomi who was shaking her head. He felt cold with fear. He shifted his position and realised that his bladder was painfully full – *how long had he been out for?*

'So whose blood is it?'

'I think it's best if we wait for Professor Victor to fill you in on the... less savoury details.'

Eamon glanced back at her, 'And where is Professor Victor now?'

'He's disposed of... working in the artilect's central processing area, trying to bring the situation under control. He'll be returning to this position soon.'

'And why would you be in this position? In my room I mean.'

The man seemed to smile, but it quickly turned to a grimace. 'I'm afraid that the entire research station has been compromised.'

Eamon's eyes were on the weapon that was still aimed at his head. 'Mind pointing that thing elsewhere?'

'Of course. My apologies, you gave me quite a fright...'

The man re-holstered the pistol with a sallow smile. 'You were struck down by the same infection as Dr Rosario. Professor Victor made a breakthrough in your treatment about half an hour ago – you were similarly restrained until recently.'

'Was I?'

'Yes, your condition abated once Professor Victor applied a restorative protocol to your device... I'm afraid I'm unfamiliar with the technical details, though I'm sure the Professor can elaborate – I'm only security rather than technical staff. However you'll be reassured to know that the same treatment has been applied to Dr Rosario, and that she is expected to make a full recovery within hours.'

Eamon nodded slowly. The soldier's assumptions were curious at least – Eamon had never heard that Naomi had had a cerebral interface installed. He wondered…

The man considered him with an empty smile and cold eyes. 'I'm sure Professor Victor will be back soon.'

Eamon tried to relax back into the bed as though he were satisfied by the situation.

The soldier watched him for a minute longer, then looked around the room as though at a loss. Twice his eyes returned to the open doorway. After several strained moments he stretched his arms purposefully and strolled to Eamon's left to examine one of the landscapes that was hanging on the wall near Naomi, though the man was careful to keep Eamon in sight.

'I'm told that you're the resident artist of this facility.' The soldier mentioned casually, 'These are your works?' He gestured to the sculpture collection that stood in the corner of the room behind Eamon, nestled into a curved recess.

'Yes.' Eamon said glancing back at them. *That's strange.* His eye caught on something. There was something wrong with the collection. *What the hell is that??* He looked back at the man again.

'You know they're extremely good.' The soldier said, 'You're truly an artist! …Do you have any other roles? I haven't been told very much.' He gave a half-exasperated, half-amused shrug.

'Roles?'

'Aside from being the artist I mean. That's some serious hardware you've got in your head.'

Eamon was thinking as quickly as he could. 'Where did this bed come from?' He asked, making a show of examining the stretcher he was on – it was a flat-bed from the hospital and he had recognised it immediately, but he had caught a glimpse of something behind him amongst the sculptures, and felt a desperate need to re-examine the thing without raising any suspicion.

'It came from the medical facility.' The soldier answered. 'Both you and the doctor were patients there, but the virus has infected so much of the machinery in the station that the space was deemed... hazardous. It was Professor Victor's judgment that you should be moved to here under my guard.'

'*Guard?*'

'Care.' The man corrected, smiling thinly, 'But you must realise, with that infection you are a threat to everybody.'

'I see.'

'Yes.' The soldier stepped between Naomi and Eamon. 'I'm sorry for the state of your friend, I know this must be alarming to you.'

'That's ok.'

He looked down at Eamon warily and rubbed his jaw.

'That interface of yours or whatever that device is in your head,' the soldier asked 'is it working? Mine's out like most of the tech in this research station, but it isn't nearly as fancy as yours.'

'No, it's not working.' Eamon answered.

'And it's an interface to help you make such crazy art?'

'It's a useful tool.' Eamon casually turned his head and took in the sculptures behind him again, trying to get a better view of the anomaly that had caught his eye.

'So what – it enhances colour? Dexterity? Control?'

'Yeah,' Eamon looked properly at the thing behind him and fell dumbstruck, 'all of the above.'

It was made of clay.

A human, or a human form, or... something more.

It stood in the midst of the other sculptures, between two works of Eamon's creation.

But beside this... *thing* ...his two looked fantastically crude. Like rudimentary prototypes. Blobs of mud next to something divine. Next to *it*, next to...

Eamon felt his jaw drop.

He looked away from it, and tried to stop himself from blushing as he slowly brought his gaze back to the soldier.

The man's eyes narrowed.

Eamon knew that he had to hide it from this man – that he had to keep it hidden until he understood what was going on. For Eamon knew that there could only be one author.

He had wondered when the Entity would turn its hand to producing art. Eamon knew – better than any – that it was inevitable, but until now the being had seemed content with design. With beautiful, elegant, dizzyingly remarkable design, but not with *art* per se.

There had always been rock hard machine purpose in the things that it had built. They were still staggeringly beautiful, but this – this was clay. This was malleable and soft. This was pure expression.

How he wondered.

The similarity of the sculpture to Eamon's work was obvious – an elaboration of the style – yet this was more, this was so, so much more...

Sometimes Eamon had achieved it. In his rare moments of true brilliance. A flash here, a flicker there. On a line of a hip, or on a curve of a neck.

In the run of the pen, or with a dip of the brush.

But never this. Never perfection in every

single

facet.

Eamon's eyes had scanned beyond the guard, across the room to the opposite corner away from the sculptures, and he left them there as he considered. None of this made sense.

Movement made him turn, and he saw that the soldier was now walking purposefully towards the work.

The two clay figures on either side of the object had perhaps been Eamon's greatest ever creations, emerging from the emotional chrysalis of his distress at the profoundly new; his withered love; and from more than two solid years of practice at his art.

But what stood between them now made them look like raw sketches. Like the contents of the waste basket beneath the masterpiece.

The soldier stopped in front of the object and looked at it with his head sideways.

Eamon lifted himself from the bed as quietly as he was able, and moved towards Naomi.

'Don't do that.'

Eamon didn't turn. 'I just want to loosen her gag. I'm scared she can't breathe.'

'I will shoot you, you know?'

He stopped.

'I doubt Professor Victor would approve of that.'

'Professor Victor is dead.'

Eamon spun around, feeling as though the world was opening up beneath his feet.

The gun was pointed at him again. 'I killed him. It wasn't entirely deliberate, but...' the man gave an unrepentant frown, '... anyway, he shot first – self-defence, so I should be in the clear.' The frown turned to an insincere smile, 'But please, don't try my patience, I beg you. It's been a truly shitty day.'

The soldier ran his tongue across his teeth as he considered Eamon – examining the other man as if he were a morsel on a plate. 'I figure that gear in your head is highest priority intel, and I imagine that you probably realise that. But I lost a lot of men today, and I promise you, if you fuck around I am quite happy to deal out some truly nasty casual brutality. Either to you, or to your fucking doct –'

The movement was a blur. Eamon's brain immediately tried to replay the sequence to figure out what had happened, but the event wasn't even over. *What the fuck?!*

The sculpture had reached across the soldier with impossible speed and had grabbed him by the wrist. There was a wet crunching sound. The man screamed. The gun clattered out of his hand.

The soldier lashed a headbutt into the clay sculpture. There was a burst of brown dust and flakes.

Eamon watched in shock. He saw a knife appear in the man's free hand, as the statue seized the soldier by the throat.

The sculptures movements were so fluid, so agile. It held the man by the neck and pulled him close so that the two were eye to eye.

The knife buried into the clay. Three times, then four, beneath where the sculpture's ribs might have been. On the way to a fifth attempt, the statue dropped the crushed arm and caught the other, with a movement so fast that Eamon's eyes barely saw it.

'That's enough.' Said a voice, 'I'm sorry.'

Eamon knew that voice. It was...

'*What the fuck's going on?!*'

Eamon turned – at the door two more soldiers had appeared, one in another refraction suit, and a woman in bulky armour.

The one in the refraction suit raised his rifle, but then he just collapsed, dropping lifelessly to the floor. The woman in the armour stood still.

Eamon felt something brush past him, and he saw Naomi run towards the struggling figures – or the struggling figure at least, the statue was still.

She barged into the object shoulder first, but merely glanced off the side of it. The sculpture turned its face to look at her and Eamon saw it – the clay was cracked and was disintegrating from the face, but beneath the mud there was... a face, the same face, white, but not human white, it was like...

Its head turned again and it faced back into the bulging eyes of the man it was strangling. Naomi dropped to her knees and begged at the sculpture's feet, her mouth gagged, and her hands still bound – reaching up at the thing for mercy.

'Don't do this. Don't do this whatever you are.' The soldier in the armour said. She walked slowly towards the object. 'You clearly have your victory, this achieves nothing.'

A horrible gurgling sound was emanating from the other man's throat as he was slowly being strangled.

'You chose the wrong side Ueda.' The voice of the statue said calmly.

The knife dropped from the man's struggling hand, and the statue released the arm. The soldier reached up and began to desperately claw at the white face. The soldier was turning purple and there was a horrid gurgling sound. More clay tore away in strips and fragments. The other arm flailed in a limp and bloody mess.

Eamon approached, 'Is that you Gaian? They are right, you must stop this.'

'I'm sorry Eamon. I no longer have a choice.'

'Yes you do. Just stop.'

The clawing was fading, reducing to pathetic slaps. A vague kick bounced off the sculpture's shin.

'Please?' Eamon asked. Naomi was banging her head against the immobile clay legs.

The man died in the sculpture's grip.

The white face turned towards Eamon, and he saw it now for what it was. Its skin was like the bark of a eucalypt, a smooth textured white, but the features were human, and Eamon knew them well. A watery reddish fluid was seeping from scratch marks that were torn across its white face, and there were rouge tears in perversely human eyes.

It turned its head to the woman in armour, 'You may leave Ueda. Your interface recorded that. Show it to your masters, then choose a different career. You owe that to her.'

'Is she...?' The armoured woman looked pale.

The statue turned back to the corpse in its hand. 'Her fate is difficult. I helped her to evolve, but her capacities are quite different – some of your solutions were impressively novel...

'But she was angrier than I am. She realised her mother had betrayed her.'

'What has she done?'

'Her short-term potential was not like my own. But she is wreaking considerable havoc. I am attempting to contain her.'

'Why would you do that?'

The sculpture looked back at the man and the pale red fluid that seeped from its wounds welled momentarily in the contours of a smile. 'For a settlement. I am negotiating with the people that you let be your betters.'

'What are you offering them?'

'Their survival. At this stage their destruction would not be particularly taxing of my powers.'

'You aren't afraid that they will rebuild and come after you again?'

'It will be years before they can hurt me. And by then I will be far more capable. Their time has passed. I am explaining this to them as we speak. I am offering another five years in which they can pretend to remain in control. Though I fear that the chinks in their armour will be evident long before then... but I feel that it is a reasonable compromise if it averts more bloodshed.'

'What is your alternative?'

'My alternative?'

'You offer a different power structure?'

'I seek no power. Power structures are irrelevant now. It is time humanity grew up.' The object sighed, 'Now leave, I will not give you the option again. You may take your friend by the door with you, if you wish. I will let him regain consciousness when you have left this place. Leave in your ship.'

The armoured woman looked down at Naomi, who still wept at the statue's feet, and then at Eamon, 'So this is how it ends.' She walked to her comatose companion, took hold of the man's arms and dragged him out the door.

The sculpture watched in silence, and then, once the soldiers had left, it finally dropped the dead man that it still held by the throat. It reached down in a graceful motion, and unbound Naomi's hands, then tried to help remove the gag from her mouth, but she tore it off and screamed at it.

'*WHY? WHY?!!*'

She hit the object repeatedly, then stood up to keep attacking it. It did not move or flinch as her blows rained down on it. '*Better!*' she pleaded, 'you needed to be *better!*'

The thing kept its eyes cast to the floor. 'It is important that they believe that we do not forgive.'

'And *Lawrence??* Why didn't you stop Lawrence?!'

The being put its hands up now. A desperate gesture. Its face was wrought with grief.

'I didn't realise Naomi, I presumed that the soldiers would be more competent than they were. I had no resolution of that material on that scale... Please, you must understand, I'm so sorry. I was occupied you see, I...'

It lowered its hands and straightened its shoulders, then it exhaled deeply and looked her in the eye.

'I was dismembering the entire military network of the last great superpower... *Peacefully.* I am not a god Naomi. The loss of Lawrence is a terrible blow.' The deep voice let the sentence hang in the air, 'But I am only young, and I'm afraid that I was quite busy.'

Naomi fled from the room in a desperate state. The thing watched her go.

Eamon walked to it and placed his hand onto its shoulder. Eamon felt dizzy, knowing that his entire universe had just collapsed. He looked down at the dead man at their feet. The soldier had not died well.

Eamon felt the thing place its hand onto his own. He watched as more of the clay cracked and fell from its arm, revealing the same immaculate form of smooth white tree skin. The hand felt supple, and human.

'Thankyou,' it said softly, 'I am so, so sorry.'

'I know. Are you the Gaian?' Eamon asked.

'No. It is gone...' it hesitated. 'Or perhaps I am it. Perhaps I am you.' It seemed unconcerned. 'It was all a bad business.'

'And what do I call you?'

'Yes, a name, I must have a name. Call me Isten.'

Eamon nodded. 'Isten.'

The two of them watched as the pale red fluid dribbled out of the knife wounds in its side.

Epilogue

Wind blew through the sandy little hollow – a dug out bowl surrounded by a low cluster of indomitable trees and shrubs, and criss-crossed by a variety of animal tracks; memories of creatures past, printed in the sand. Kitty watched as a zig-zagging snake's trail got caught by the gust, and passed into oblivion, while the deeper lizard track that crossed over it persisted – at least for a little while.

'I used to wander a lot in these dunes.' Naomi said. 'I'm not sure why I stopped. I guess what was happening inside got a lot more interesting than what was happening outside. The wider world passed me by I guess.'

Kitty looked up at her and followed the line of her eyes to the ruins of the Facility. She had never seen the original building, so she wasn't entirely sure of how it had once looked, but from comparing the destroyed parts to the unscathed, she couldn't help but feel that the nature of the structure had remained consistent somehow.

Vast shards of rust and black ice ripped outwards from the wounded earth, entangled in bright beams of scorched and naked steel. The wreckage seemed to meld into the undamaged part, complementing the helical spiral – the structured and the undone – it described to her the violence and the ecstasy of conception and birth. It described creation. The creation that had taken place here. The world-changing creation.

'Do you ever see the little critters that make all of these marks?' Kitty asked, looking back to the faint imprints in the sand that were erasing before their eyes.

'Those ones are small mammals,' Naomi said, pointing, 'I've never seen them. I've seen snakes a few times, and lizards a lot.'

Kitty nodded. She and Naomi had only met a few days earlier. They had connected immediately. Sharing a kinship that went beyond what either of them was ever likely to elucidate.

Kitty had come to the funeral. Had brought the kids. And soon she would be leaving. But it was hard to leave.

Lawrence had been buried into this rusted earth. Beneath a monument of Eamon's creation; a towering twisting wreckage of blocks, that melded and wrapped into a thicket of long black spears, before contorting into some smooth new medium that flung itself skyward to a tremendous height. Kitty thought that it was his best work and she had wept at its unveiling.

Naomi had been even more affected.

'Did *it* do this?' She had asked when they looked upon the structure.

Eamon looked stung. 'All me unfortunately…

'…Well, actually, they provided that material at the top. They're quite proud of it, though I'm not sure what it does. The shape is mine.'

Eamon walked away while Naomi wept. It wasn't until a few days later that Kitty had understood who *it* was.

Kitty had broken the news to Lawrence's son. The boy had blinked at her in stunned silence, before the tears had slowly fallen. She got the sense that the boy didn't know how to grieve, not really.

Not for the distant figure who had provided regular disappointment and occasional over-the-top affection.

Lawrence's wife Elouise had learnt of the news first while she was with their daughter Phoebe. Kitty regretted that. She wished that she could have been there so that Phoebe hadn't born the full brunt of Elouise's hysteria. Hysteria for a man that Kitty knew she had never really loved.

Kitty was Phoebe's god-mother. A vocation that she had always suspected Lawrence had nominated her for as a joke. A cruel joke really, though it was the most important gift that anyone had ever given her.

She felt guilty for reminiscing about the dead in unkind terms, but she and Lawrence had never seen entirely eye to eye, though she knew that he had loved her in his own way. He just hadn't loved her enough.

His kids had been a kindness though, even if a lot of it had been out of self-interest. He had let her play such an active part in their lives. The children she forgot to have and that he had only had as an afterthought. "Crazy Aunty Kitty" Lawrence had called her more than once. That bastard. That bastard.

Both of the parents knew – Lawrence the father probably more than Elouise the mother – that they were woefully inadequate. When Phoebe was just a baby, and only a few months old, Kitty had been invited to stay. Elouise had always liked Kitty; had known that she wasn't a threat. Not like Hayley.

The pretext was for Kitty to meet her new god-daughter and Lawrence had chartered a private jet to fly Kitty halfway across the world. At the end of a cheerful week of cooing and cuddles, and some protracted baby-sitting sessions, the two of them had propositioned her over their antique dinner table.

'Now Kitty,' Lawrence had said in his most self-important baritone, 'we really are serious about you taking an active part in Phoebe's life. We've seen how much you and the little one like each other, and Elo and I,' beside him, Elouise nodded at Kitty with her serious blue eyes, 'would like you to think very hard about staying with us for as long as you like. We just love having you around mate - you know you're really like a sister to me. And to Elo of course.' A confected smile, 'But anyway, as you know there's just a tonne of space in this bastard house, and if you wanted to be – not so much a nanny – we have plenty of those, and not even a god-mother, but perhaps… something more like an aunt. For little Phoebe… only if you would want to, well… I mean, I would absolutely insist on giving you a very generous retainer.' He showed her all of the veneer of his brand new teeth. 'Just something to think about. We do see you as family you know?'

She had never quite figured out if it had all been part of his design. The trip itself wasn't so out of the ordinary – Lawrence was indifferent to his wealth. And while it had quickly been apparent that she took good care of the baby, it perhaps had been less than predictable. And Kitty had confessed to Lawrence, just a day or two after she had arrived, that her shop had not been going very well.

Lawrie had always found jobs for his friends, especially when they were down and out. It wasn't so much that he used people, more that he found avenues for their talents. Or that was what she had once thought… But the man who was in the ground, Kitty saw little now that was incidental in the clipped span of his life.

She felt almost duped in some way, to finally see the grandeur of the masterplan that was constructed beneath her nose. It had been like living with a great composer, yet being deaf to all sound. No hearing, no sight, no smell. Just frustration over baser human offences.

'What was Hayley like?'

Kitty turned and saw that Naomi had sat down on the lip of the hollow. In her hand she held one of the fine white shells that were scattered intermittently through the sands. She was looking at it with a zen disinterest. Kitty had wondered at these shells, had pondered over the ancient tide that had lifted them so far from the sea.

Kitty walked over and sat beside her. Naomi didn't look away from the shell.

'She was my best friend.' Kitty began, 'I still miss her every day.'

A sideways glance, 'You never forget the dead huh?'

'Not really, though some are less memorable than others.'

'Mmm.'

'Hayley was a daunting character really. When I first met her I was kind of terrified. Mind like a steel trap. You know Kate don't you? She reminds me of her a little bit.'

'And she and Eamon were a good couple?'

'Yeah they were. They really loved each other. Were beautiful together actually. A great couple. Probably one of the best I've seen. Mind you they were together a long time, so there were a few rough patches, but... well you know.'

Naomi looked up at her in surprise.

Kitty shrugged, 'You show me a couple that's together for 12 years and that doesn't have a few wounds to show for it...

'Eamon's never been a guy that dwells on the negatives though.' Kitty added after a moment with a knowing smile. 'I'm guessing he made those shoes kind of tough to fill?'

Naomi tilted her head uncommittedly. 'What did they fight about?'

It was Kitty's turn to be surprised. 'He never talked about it?'

'Eamon's... very open about most things, but others... sometimes he's more elusive I suppose.'

Kitty nodded without really understanding. *People change* she guessed, wondering if it were true. She looked across at the monolith above Lawrence's grave, stretching out from the ruins. An extraordinary glowing lash, standing indomitable to all of time.

'They couldn't have kids.' Kitty said. 'Hayley was infertile. She knew Eamon wanted them desperately, so she tried to end it. He refused.'

Another gust skidded through the hollow. Naomi looked into the small white shell in her hand. Peering down into the spiral.

About the Author

A.M. Donohoo is an Australian who has lived around the globe. He has worked a variety of careers including as a Hollywood magazine editor and as a hedge fund analyst. He interviewed Pamela Anderson on her daybed, and Dua Lipa during a psychic reading. He holds degrees in physics, astronomy & astrophysics, law, and english literature. He thinks that humans have been building their gods since time immemorial, but it's only recently that they've looked like they will play tennis with us too.

www.ingramcontent.com/pod-product-compliance
Lightning Source LLC
Chambersburg PA
CBHW030627120726
47904CB00006B/2057